WHY DID SHE ALWAYS SAY
MORE THAN SHE INTENDED
TO THIS GENTLEMAN?

"I should have warned you, perhaps," Lord Carrigan said as he flicked his reins, "that it is not the customary thing for a young lady to appear alone in public with a gentleman."

Emily tossed her head arrogantly. "I have decided to obey the rules which are sensible and disregard those which are not," she told him . . .

They were, in fact, attracting some attention, particularly as they reached the vicinity of St. James Park and the fashionable mall.

"I think it is possible that you have not quite decided what posture to adopt," Lord Carrigan told her. "No doubt your natural impulses are warring with the practices which the *haut ton* imposes. I saw that at once the first evening that we met. I went too far and shocked you but I did not realize that you were so . . ."

"Innocent?" Emily demanded.

Other Avon Books Coming Soon by
Valerie Bradstreet

THE IVORY FAN

THE
FORTUNE WHEEL

VALERIE BRADSTREET

AVON
PUBLISHERS OF BARD, CAMELOT, DISCUS AND FLARE BOOKS

THE FORTUNE WHEEL is an original publication of Avon Books. This work has never before appeared in book form.

AVON BOOKS
A division of
The Hearst Corporation
959 Eighth Avenue
New York, New York 10019

First Avon Printing, August, 1981

AVON TRADEMARK REG. U.S. PAT. OFF. AND IN OTHER COUNTRIES, MARCA REGISTRADA, HECHO EN U.S.A.

Printed in the U.S.A.

10 9 8 7 6 5 4 3 2 1

*for Kinley
with love*

CHAPTER ONE

"Emily, my dear, you really should try to keep yourself from fretting," Lady Fairfield declared, rubbing her plump cheeks with vermillion, until she created a blush of the sort any girl of eighteen would have envied. "Cheerfulness is the most important thing, I always say. Phoebe will agree with me, I know."

"Oh, yes, Mama!" Phoebe declared, red curls spinning as she revolved like a plump top before the pier glass, the better to admire her new green and silver ball gown, which sported an agreeable degree of décolletage. "If you have taught me anything, it is that *everything* comes right in the end "

Emily considered her aunt and cousin with an expression of frustration on her pretty face. Lady Fairfield and her daughter were both rotund and merry, while Emily was slim and serious, seemingly quite unaware of what a lovely sight she made, sitting on the window seat of her aunt's dressing room in her blue, sprigged, muslin polonaise gown, her black curls half-hidden by a frilly mobcap. Since she had come up to London from the country two weeks ago to join her aunt at her home in Cavendish Square, Emily had constantly been amazed at the boundless optimism with which both mother and daughter greeted what appeared to Emily to be one intolerable situation after another. Not only could the two find silver linings where Emily was certain none existed, but they were adept at making triumphs out of what appeared to be absolute defeats.

"You will not find my sister to be the practical sort," Emily's father had told her by way of preparation. "Still, she is good-hearted, which is the most important thing, and she writes that she is eager to see to your coming-out."

Since it had been Lady Fairfield's whim, after having been widowed, to reside a good part of the time on the Continent, Emily had had only the faintest recollection of either her aunt or of her cousins, Phoebe and her brother Jeremy. Granted that when Emily's own mother had been alive, she could frequently be heard bewailing the feck-lessness with which Lady Fairfield dealt with financial matters.

"You have bailed your sister out too frequently, my dear," she would protest to Emily's father. "How do you expect her to learn to deal with harsh reality if you con-tinually put things right?"

But the Squire, as he was called, had not listened then and the passing years had brought no change, even though his own fortune had been dealt a blow by certain unwise investments he had made on the Exchange.

"Who would have thought that all three ships would sink?" Emily had heard him muttering shortly before she had left the shabby manor house in Kent, which her fa-ther had inherited from his own father, who had been the second son of a marquess. "All that silver at the bottom of the Atlantic. Ah, well. Such things will happen, even though it is a pity. We all turn about on fortune's wheel."

And so there had been hints, but Emily had not been acquainted with the full force of her father's rapidly ap-proaching impecuniosity until, the very day after she had arrived in London, she had been visited by his solicitor, a certain Mr. Drew, who had warned her, in no uncertain terms, of impending disaster.

"Your father is a very generous man, Miss Brooke," he had informed her, settling his periwig more securely in position with the knob end of his cane and squinting at her though the small, round spectacles that he wore almost at the very end of his thin nose. "Combine that admirable quality with an unerring lack of business sense, and you are courting trouble. There was no great harm in it, you see, until he began to dip into his capital. But, now, I am afraid he may be in for it, if you will excuse the expres-sion."

The immediate purpose of Mr. Drew's visit had been to

inform Emily that the allowance she could expect to receive while she was in London must, perforce, be substantially decreased. But, encouraged by her practicality and general good sense, the solicitor had gone on to urge her to do whatever she thought she could in order to deal with what he termed to be a very sorry situation.

"Your father intends to come to town a bit later in the Season, I believe," he had said, making another attempt to deal with the recalcitrant periwig. "Perhaps you could take that opportunity to argue prudence, for I scarcely dare to think what may happen when he next approaches the Exchange."

Upon Emily's assurance that she would do whatever she could to assist, the little man had gone on to propose that she deal with her aunt in a similar fashion.

"No one could be more agreeable than Lady Fairfield," he had assured her, "but I do not think I put it too strongly when I suggest that I have never seen anyone with so little business sense. Her husband, the late Viscount, left her with little enough, and, as you may well know, your father has settled her arrears a score of times. Against my advice, I might add. Against my strong advice. She could manage well enough if she would only practice some economy, and now that you are living in her house, you might be able to exert some influence."

So much inflamed had Mr. Drew's imagination become, by dint of having found a sensible member of the family at last, that he had, indeed, become quite frank and intimate before their interview had come to an end.

"Of course, it goes without saying that you must marry money, my dear Miss Brooke," he had concluded. "You will forgive me if I say that, endowed as you are with such a degree of natural beauty, you should easily be able to make an excellent match. Yes, yes! An excellent match, indeed! I'm certain that your father must depend upon it."

The notion was as fresh to Emily as it was disagreeable. Never once had it been so much as hinted at that her father's fate might rest on her slim shoulders. But, having seen Mr. Drew to the door, she could quite see the strength of his argument, and it had not been a heartening revelation.

As a consequence, Emily had turned her attention to her aunt's predicament, which had soon manifested itself with so much clarity that it was difficult for her to believe that Lady Fairfield could not have seen it before. But, whenever she raised the subject of practical considerations, her aunt insisted that, far from anything being wrong, she was living in the best of all possible worlds.

The sound of her aunt's voice ended Emily's reveries.

"I am certain that you must be mistaken about what is happening in the kitchen, my dear," she said now, allowing her abigail Nelly, a pert-faced miss who always seemed to be smiling at a secret joke, to begin to wrap her turban.

Emily shook her head in a warning fashion and did not reply. She had begun this discussion when Nelly had been out of the room, and, given certain circumstances that she knew she must inform her aunt of in good time, she did not think it the best of wisdom to talk about the servants in front of one of their number.

"La!" Phoebe cried, ceasing her revolutions before the mirror and coming to rest on the hearth rug in her usual disingenuous manner. "You must be mistaken, Emily. Why, I have heard Cook say any number of times that no one could possibly exercise more economy than she does. Not to put too fine a point on it, I do not know what we would do without her."

"How well you do the winding, Nelly!" Lady Fairfield congratulated her abigail. "And now you must go and find the two ostrich feathers, the ones I had dyed blue. They are in my bedchamber somewhere. Indeed, I think one of them may be behind the wardrobe, of all the curious places for it to have got to."

As soon as the door of the dressing room had closed behind the smiling Nelly, Emily took up her interrupted argument.

"The fact is, Aunt," she said in a low voice, "I think you should keep a closer eye on household matters. It is just possible that you are letting your servants take advantage of you in certain ways. For instance, I have noticed—"

"I do not know where that silver brooch can have gotten to," Lady Fairfield said cheerfully, digging about in her carved-ivory jewelry box and then, clearly unable to find the ornament, emptying the contents on her dressing table.

"You remember the brooch I mean, Phoebe, don't you?" she continued. "The one your brother gave me on my last birthday. Emily, my dear, I did not mean to interrupt you. And I do think you are wrong about the servants. They are all so very amiable, so willing to please. Indeed, I do not know how I could get along without a single one of them. And I prefer to trust the people about me, you see. Life is so much simpler that way, and I do not care to worry."

It was clear to Emily that her aunt would prefer not to hear any evidence to the contrary and that it would do little good to recount anything she had observed, including the fact that Mrs. Burbain, the cook, appeared to order enough in the way of stores to feed a regiment, if the troop of tradespeople with loaded wagons who came to the back on Thursdays when her aunt and Phoebe regularly played whist at Lady Warren's were any proof. Besides, before she could say another word, Nelly drifted back into the room, trailing the blue ostrich feathers behind her on the floor. A glint of late afternoon sunlight chose that moment to dart through the window and strike the silver ornament pinned to the abigail's muslin neckerchief.

Emily could not suppress a sigh. She had not been in this house two days before she had suspected that Nelly was responsible for the extraordinary number of articles that her aunt and Phoebe discovered missing. Indeed, it was almost unheard of for them to dress for any entertainment without finding that some trinket or other that they thought of wearing had been lost.

"Oh, well, I will simply buy another," was Lady Fairfield's usual response. "I think there must be a mischievous little fairy somewhere in his house, who delights in spiriting things away."

Since Nelly was the only person besides herself and her cousins and the upstairs maid to have access to her aunt's bedchamber, Emily had been quick to overlook the possibilities of acquisitive fairies in favor of more reasonable explanations. But, given the combination of her aunt's reluctance to hear any fault found with her servants and their apparent dedication to her service, Emily had hesitated in the past. Now, however, she could not keep from commenting on the fact that Nelly seemed to be wearing a brooch very like the one her aunt was missing.

"Why, I declare, Miss!" the abigail cried. "Her Lady-ship never minds if I deck myself up any way I fancy while I'm waiting on her, and this silver brooch caught my eye today. I had no way of knowing you'd be looking for it, did I, Ma'am?"

Having made her protest, she let a slippery smile slide slowly across her lips as she surveyed Emily triumphantly. And, indeed, she had every reason to do just that, for Lady Fairfield was off on a perfect torrent of assurance that Nelly was quite right and that she always encouraged her to try on bits and pieces of her jewelry or ribbons or anything she liked.

"Why, sometimes," she declared, "the gel looks such a treat in something or other that I give it to her straight-away. Isn't that so, Phoebe?"

"You are generous to a fault, Mama," her daughter cried, "and I try to be the same whenever possible."

Emily lowered her head and closed her eyes, but not before she had been treated to the sight of Nelly unpin-ning the brooch with perfect equanimity and placing it on the dressing table as though that had been what she had meant to do with it all the time.

"You look as though you have a megrim, Emily," she heard her aunt declare. "Run and fetch the powders that the doctor prescribed for me, Nelly, do. I believe I lent the packet to Danvers the other night. Do you remember, Phoebe? We were on our way to Almack's, and he was just seeing us out when he complained of such a dreadful headache that I told him he must take some of my medi-cine straightaway. I expect he quite forgot to return it."

With Nelly once more out of the room, Emily struggled with the decision of whether to continue what would seem to be a fruitless line of accusations or to give way to her aunt's incurable optimism. The generosity her aunt had shown to her butler was another case in point, for Emily had reason to think that Danvers was exercising the most amazing fraud of all.

"You will think it strange, no doubt," her aunt had said in her cheerful way that first time they had sat down to sup together, "to find tin knives and forks and spoons upon the table, but Danvers tells me that not only does it take up too much of his time to polish silver, but that it is the better part of wisdom to put it safely away, London being so full of thieves and silver melted down so easily. I declare that I was grateful to Danvers to think of hiding it away. Indeed, he is so cautious about it that he will not even tell me where it is."

"Danvers would do anything for us!" Phoebe declared with enthusiasm. "And so would all the other servants! Only fancy, some of them came to us without recommendation, which is, no doubt, why they are so grateful."

"I always think it is a mistake to put too much confidence in the word of others," Lady Fairfield declared, tucking her ostrich feathers in her turban in a becoming fashion and using the silver brooch to fasten them in place. "Why, you will recall, Phoebe, that Lady Marshford told me that Bert, our footman, could not be trusted across the room, which was, I thought, a curious way of putting it. And only think how satisfactory we have found him!"

Lady Fairfield was a rotund, little woman whose face had been so much creased by smiling that there was scarcely a smooth surface to be seen. However that might be, she had fine brown eyes, which were set off to advantage by a certain protrusion, and a charming snubbed nose that suited her disposition. It had been her good fortune, she often said, to have a youthful mirror in her daughter Phoebe.

"We're as much alike as two peas in a pod," she often said, "except for a certain difference in age, which, given our relationship, is only to be expected."

And with that, she and Phoebe both would break into trills of laughter just as they were doing now at the very thought that anyone could mistrust their footman Bert, and suddenly it was necessary for Emily to fight the insane temptation to join them. Granting that such a degree of cheerfulness could be contagious, she must be careful for all their sakes not to lose sight of grim reality.

CHAPTER TWO

Lady Fairfield was fond of saying that no one could want a better son than Jeremy, and Emily supposed that, if this estimate were based exclusively on her cousin's disposition, the claim could be made that Jeremy might well deserve to be doted on by a fond mama. But if his habits were to be considered, the young gentleman was revealed in not quite such a glowing light. Indeed, it might well be said that he was rapidly becoming an idle fop—a beau, a man-about-town, a dandy. So busy was he, whether at his club or Almack's or Tattersall's or any of the other spots that attracted bloods and macaronies, that Emily had seen very little of him since her arrival, but what she had seen had not been reassuring. In fact, when she encountered him in the drawing room that evening while she waited for her aunt and Phoebe to join her on their way to a soiree at Lady Courtiney's, she was not as certain as she should be what to say to him.

Conversation presented no problem to Jeremy, however, as Emily soon discovered. Her cousin was considerably taller than his mother, but equally rotund, with the same protruding brown eyes. But he was not cheerful. Indeed, it came as a considerable relief to Emily that, instead of smiling when she joined him, he gave her a baleful glance and demanded, quite abruptly, whether or not his cravat was wrapped too high. And since, in matter of fact, he had made such an elaborate to-do of it that his mouth could scarcely be seen, Emily was obliged to say that it might be just as well if he allowed more of his lower face to be seen. Whereupon, he had undertaken to deal with the problem then and there to the tune of much impatient muttering and several oaths of such an original variety that Emily made a pretense of looking out the window at the street, which was crowded with carriages conveying the members of the haut monde to wherever they had decided to make their evening's entertainment.

"Damme, is that better then?" Jeremy demanded, and Emily, deciding that it was the better part of wisdom not to offer further criticism, assured him that he looked the very heart and soul of style, despite the fact that privately she thought his red, high-heeled shoes a bit fanciful and the patches on his face too numerous by far.

"That's all right, then," the young gentleman declared in a self-satisfied manner, striking a pose, with one elbow on the mantel of the fireplace. "Tell me, Cousin, are you enjoying London? It is a delightful place, I think, although Paris is more exciting. That was where we most often stayed when we were abroad, you know. It suited my mother to be some place where she did not speak the language well."

Emily would have asked him to explain what was, after all, a most enigmatic remark, had it not been for the fact that what little contact she had had with him before had given her good reason to believe that he specialized in bons mots, clever sayings which often seemed to be contradictions. Knowing that amusement was the desired response, she smiled obligingly and allowed the monologue to continue, wondering as she did so whether Jeremy could be convinced to put aside his own self-indulgence long enough to give some serious consideration to the fact that his mama was doing nothing to keep herself from teetering on the brink of economic disaster. But, having learned that her cousin had "dipped a trifle" at White's that afternoon in a game of deep basset, and that he intended to return to gambling this evening as soon as he could get away from the soiree, Emily came to the conclusion that a lecture from her on the subject of economy would, no doubt, strike a sour note.

"Odd rot it," Jeremy declared, striking still another pose with his arms crossed at the level of his chest, "I'll be a gudgeon if I'd show my face at Lady Courtiney's at all if the dear old pippin upstairs would not be chafed about it. She's always on at me to find some strumpet or other to want to marry, and, as a consequence, I must turn respectable once a week, at least."

Emily knew enough of her cousin to think that a good part of what he said was as empty of meaning as steam rising from a kettle. It was one thing for him to call his mother a pippin in front of Emily, but he would not be quite so disrespectful as to address Lady Fairfield in such a manner to her face. And as for his pretense of living a wild and dissipated life, Emily thought that the young gentlemen with whom he chose to spend his time were guilty of little more than self-indulgence and a tendency to drink and gamble to excess. Certainly, Lady Fairfield found nothing to keep herself from describing Jeremy as a jewel of young manhood—all of which often caused her listeners to shake their heads in disbelief.

And, indeed, when Lady Fairfield came hurrying into the drawing room a few minutes later, with Phoebe close behind, nothing could be faulted in the clear delight she showed that Jeremy was to attend them. No doubt, because her gown had brown and yellow stripes, she looked exceedingly like a happy bumblebee, as she buzzed about the room, gathering up her reticule from one corner where she had dropped it earlier and her pelisse from another.

"I know a certain young lady who will be thrown into ecstasy to see you there tonight, my dear!" she exclaimed, pausing for a moment to chuck a disgusted Jeremy under the chin as though he were still a baby. "To tell the truth, I expect there will be more than one heart beating faster. It really would be a kindness for you to make your choice among them soon, dear boy, in order that too many false hopes are not aroused. Phoebe agrees with me, I know."

"Oh, yes, Mama!" Phoebe cried. "Jeremy is all the ladies' favorite. Still, that is hardly to be wondered at, since he is so very dashing."

Jeremy's response was to scowl and, for a moment, Emily felt a smattering of pity for him, surrounded as he had been for so long by total approbation, so much of it unearned. Certainly "dashing" was not quite the word she would have chosen to describe someone of such a fleshy appearance. Perhaps even Jeremy, self-satisfied as he was, realized that "dashing" was a step too far.

In the carriage, during their ride to Grosvenor Square,

Emily's suspicions that nothing could put her aunt out of countenance were confirmed. When, at his mother's request, Jeremy described his day, he was met with overwhelming approval. Loitering in the park was translated by his proud mama into taking exercise, while an afternoon spent gambling at White's became a pleasant visit with his friends.

"Dear Jeremy is so well liked by everyone," Lady Fairfield confided in Emily as they climbed the stairs of a palatial brick house, from every window of which a candle gleamed. "Can you believe that he has never given me an anxious moment? Did you observe the style with which he is dressed tonight? So very fashionable! And his tailor's bills are reasonable in the extreme, for, as I always say, it is cheaper in the end to buy the very best."

Once their hostess had been greeted, however, and they had entered the crowded ballroom, Jeremy took the opportunity to disappear.

"No doubt he saw a friend," Lady Fairfield said cheerfully, although in the carriage she had made it quite clear that she wished to introduce him to several young ladies whose acquaintance she had recently made. "Jeremy has friends everywhere. It comes of having such an agreeable personality. Don't you agree, Phoebe?"

Phoebe was even in more of a mood to agree to anything than usual. Her round face was flushed and her protruding brown eyes glistened with excitement. There was nothing she liked better than a ball, she said, with so much emphasis that several people in their immediate vicinity turned to stare at her.

"Only see how much attention you are attracting, my dear," Lady Fairfield said, smiling broadly. "I knew that green and silver stripes would suit you."

And indeed the stripes might have suited her, Emily considered, had they gone up and down instead of around and around, with the result that her cousin's girth appeared to be increased substantially. Still, she was the sweetest-natured person Emily had ever met, aside from Lady Fairfield herself, and she found herself hoping that nothing would ever dim the incredible optimism of either of them. She even went so far as to begin to think that it would be very wrong of her to encourage them to see the world as it really was. Indeed, if the result of their cheer-

ful disregard for facts had not predicted financial disaster,
she would have dedicated herself quite willingly to the
preservation of their dreams.

These reflections were interrupted, however, by Lady
Fairfield, who was surveying the company with an air of
delight and insisting that Emily do the same.

"Is it not a brilliant assembly, my dear?" her aunt demanded, standing on her toes to see the better. "Only note
how elegant the ladies are, and there are so many handsome gentlemen about, that I declare I could not choose
among them if I were a gel again!"

Obediently, Emily looked about her and realized that
she and her aunt were seeing the company through quite
different eyes. If by "elegance" was meant the height of
fashion, then she supposed it was a deal in evidence. But
somehow she found it difficult to appreciate so many
painted faces, which looked like masks, and so much décolletage, which often revealed necks and bosoms better
left disguised. As for the gentlemen, many of those of a
certain age appeared to be tightly corseted, ofttimes
their fingers were so heavily beringed as to make their
gestures languid, and many a white-stockinged calf could
scarcely be called well-turned. Add to such unpic-
turesque details a general artificiality of manner, as to
leave sincerity in doubt in nearly every case, and she was
far from being ready to grant a general brilliance. No,
doubt, she told herself, she was being overparticular by
far. Besides, it must be that, coming from the country as
she did, she found too much to criticize.

"Dear Lady Fairfield!" two passing ladies exclaimed in
unison. "How well you look, and Phoebe is quite charming
tonight!"

And with that, they quickly went on their way, but not
before Emily heard one of them whisper something about
"Those dreadful stripes!" behind her fan. An anxious
glance at her aunt, however, assured her that neither she
nor Phoebe had heard.

"That was Lady Buckley and her sister," Lady Fairfield
said happily. "They are always so full of compliments and
always make a point of noting Phoebe's gown."

Emily dreaded to think what degree of disillusionment
would follow if something should happen to break the
roseate glass that protected her aunt and cousin from the

world. Quite suddenly, she felt she must defend them at all costs. And yet how difficult that could be, she was to realize a minute later, when Phoebe began to bounce up and down in a high state of excitement.

"I knew that he would be here, Mama!" she exclaimed. "And only think! He is coming directly this way!"

The crush was so great that, for a moment, Emily could not discover who her cousin was talking about, but seconds afterward she saw a gentleman who seemed to be moving in their direction, although with very little urgency, not to mention speed, since he seemed to stop to talk with everyone he passed.

"That is Sir Adrian Rap," Lady Fairfield whispered to Emily. "Phoebe dotes on him and so do I. We like to think he is the perfect gentleman."

Since there was plenty of time to observe Sir Adrian in his slow progress, Emily proceeded to do so, while Phoebe and her mother chattered eagerly about how fortunate it was that he was coming to ask for the first dance, which meant, no doubt, that he would take Phoebe in to supper later in the evening. The gentleman in question was older than Emily would have thought desirable. Indeed, she thought he must be nearly the age of her aunt, for his hair, which was worn in the Cadogan style with two curled rolls above the ears and a queue at the back, was grizzled. His features were good enough, if somewhat prominent to the degree that when looking at him, one was very conscious of such things as ears and nose and chin. He was of average height and wore his canary-yellow redingote with its high, standing collar and claw hammer tails with a certain flare. The only really extraordinary thing about him were his tiny feet, which were the cause of a certain peculiarity about his gait, since it was necessary for him to take twice or even triple the ordinary number of steps in order to propel himself forward. The result was that he seemed to lurch about like someone in his cups; but when he was not moving, he was dignified enough.

And arrogant. This, of course, Emily could not observe until he had reached them at last and he had declared himself very pleased to see them and delighted to meet "the lovely Miss Brooke," as he referred to Emily, with the manner of someone conferring a distinct favor. A motley lot was in attendance tonight, he assured them. Still, he had been fortunate enough to pick up a few *on dit*s, and did they know that Lady Bitbain's daughter had eloped with the groom and that Lord Leehigh had been found sleeping off a bottle of claret in the shrubbery at Vauxhall? And, all the time he talked, he kept his eyes on Emily, sometimes raising his quizzing-glass to see her all the more clearly, and breaking off his recitation of gossip now and then to murmur, "Charming. Yes, yes! Quite charming! And just down from the country, too."

It was the first time Emily had found herself treated like an objet d'art, and she did not find the sensation at all agreeable. And there was something else to worry her. The musicians were tuning up, and she had the distinct impression that Sir Adrian might very well ask her, and not her cousin, to take the floor for the first quadrille. Of course, she told herself, she might be quite mistaken. But she thought she could not bear it if her cousin were to be disappointed, and certainly it was true that Sir Adrian had not seen fit to address Phoebe after his first greeting. On and on his stories went, one more scurrilous than the last, and now he had begun to leer at Emily in such a way that she was certain that she should escape before it was too late.

"Do forgive me!" she explained when Sir Adrian next paused for breath. "I do believe I see a neighbor of ours from the country, and I must have a word with her!"

"My dear Miss Brooke!" Sir Adrian cried. "You cannot leave before I ask you . . ."

But she was gone before he could say another word, pushing her way through the scented company with very little attention to delicacy. And, in her haste, she caught the attention of a little circle of young bucks who decided to make a game of it and joined hands around her.

"Hye! Here's a pretty wench!" one cried.

"Damme, Nicholson, she is a handsome hussy, is she not?"

A tall young man who had been staring rudely through his quizzing-glass, dropped it by its ribbon and declared that he would be a rumstick if he let her get off without a kiss. At that, he tried, but Emily ducked her head to make him miss, whereupon the others taunted him by shouting "Nicholson has no aim," and other such insults. It was all too clear that they were in their cups and

Emily whirled about, glaring at them angrily. How dared they interfere with her like this? They were already attracting considerable attention and, doubtless, it would not be long before Sir Adrian would notice what was happening and come, unwelcome, to her rescue. If there was anything she did not want it was to be in his debt in any way.

"Let me pass, sir!" she demanded of the one called Nicholson. "I swear you will be the worse for it if you will not!"

"Pox upon it, she has a spirit as well as looks! Has she not, Carrigan?" he demanded.

Emily stared at him defiantly, hating the fact that as long as they surrounded her there was nothing she could do. If only she could be a man for just an hour, she told herself, she would set them on their ears.

"Dash it, here comes my brother!" a third youth with fair hair and an angelic expression that his behavior belied. "I'd be well off to stubble it from the look in his eye. But first I'll have my kiss, odd rot it, if I won't!"

But as he clasped her waist, Emily struck him such a blow with her ivory fan as to cause him to shout out in pain. In all directions, heads were turning now, and, to her horror, Emily saw Sir Adrian descending.

And, then, a stranger had taken her arm, and she was aware that the youths who had surrounded her had fled.

"I must apologize for my brother," the stranger said. "If there is anything that I can do to make up for his behavior . . ."

Emily's eyes were still trained on Sir Adrian, who was mincing as quickly as he could in her direction, quizzing-glass to his eye.

"You can ask me to dance, sir," Emily declared. "I do not care whether we take the floor or not, but I must be engaged. A gentleman is coming who will wish to take me under his protection. If you truly want to make up for your brother's scandalous behavior, you must see to it that he is not allowed to do so."

CHAPTER THREE

"My dear!" Sir Adrian cried, holding out his hands to her in his affected way. "How dreadful for you! Why, Lord Carrigan! Is it really you? 'Pon my soul, I had it on good authority only the other day that you were still in Florence."

For the first time, Emily took a good look at the stranger who had intervened on her behalf. He was very tall, and his broad shoulders seemed to strain the seams of his black satin coat. Altogether he was the sort of gentleman who looked more at home on a horse, she thought. Clearly, he spent a good deal of time out of doors, for his face was tanned. His dark hair was arranged carelessly on his forehead instead of being pulled back and into stiff curls as was the style. But the most extraordinary thing about him was his eyes, which were as black as jet and as penetrating as a knife. He did not precisely ignore Sir Adrian, but his full attention was clearly concentrated on her and Emily felt her cheeks grow warm.

"Yes, yes!" Sir Adrian went on in his fussy voice when he received no immediate answer. "No matter! You are back, I see. No doubt you have heard all about the difficulties your brother was into in your absence. Not that I would gossip about them. Never! You know me well enough to know I would never repeat what I have been told. But London is buzzing. You should be aware of that, sir. And now, my dear Miss Brooke, you must do me the pleasure of taking my arm. We will put your slight embarrassment behind you immediately and present ourselves to the dance floor. I can think of nothing that would give me more pleasure than to be your partner for the first quadrille."

It was, Emily thought, exactly as she had feared. And yet, if the stranger beside her did not help, how could she prevent being the cause of unhappiness for Phoebe? Except to say she would *not* dance. But even then he might insist on keeping her company, which would be even worse.

"I am afraid that Miss Brooke has agreed to dance this dance with me," the stranger said, in a low but resonant voice.

" 'Pon my word, sir!" Sir Adrian exclaimed. "Miss Brooke is straight up from the country and you are directly from the Continent. How does it happen you have been properly introduced?"

"We have had an improper introduction, which is just as good," Emily declared, no longer able to control her irritation. "And now I think my cousin and her mother are waiting for your return. The crush is certainly too great for them to get through. You would be doing everyone a most uncommon kindness if you would go back to them and take the word that I am quite all right and in the company of Lord Carrigan."

Clearly much against his will, Sir Adrian went mincing away on his tiny, slippered feet, pausing now and then to cast a puzzled look back over his shoulder.

"Thank you, sir," Emily said when Sir Adrian had finally disappeared. "There is no need for you to remain with me any longer, now that he is off and away. The crush is so great that I can easily keep out of sight for the remainder of the evening, if necessary."

"I must confess, Miss Brooke, you puzzle me," Lord Carrigan replied. "Clearly you are not lacking in either spirit or initiative, but why should it be necessary for anyone so lovely to hide herself away at a ball, when, I believe, just the opposite attitude is intended?"

Emily did not answer him for a moment. She was indebted to him, certainly, for saving her from the blandishments of Sir Adrian Rap, but under no conditions could she explain the precise nature of her difficulty, she thought.

"Mind you," Lord Carrigan went on with a slow smile, "I am not pressing you. You shall hide yourself away as much as you like. I only ask that you reward me by allowing that I keep your company. We do not need to dance if that is what you prefer. Indeed, I would suggest the terrace as a perfect refuge for us both."

His tone had something of the tease in it, which was enough to ruffle Emily's fur. "I expect you think that someone like myself has no more in the way of problems than to choose the color of a ribbon or the cut of a new gown," she said stiffly. "But I assure you that, in this case at least, it is not true. There is no need for you to treat me like a child, sir, for although some ladies may think such condescension is a compliment, I assure you that I do not. I can manage for myself very well indeed."

The mocking smile was still on his lips. "You were not managing quite well enough when I came along and rescued you just now," he reminded her.

Suddenly, Emily remembered something she had heard just before the youths had vanished. "One of them was your brother, sir!" she cried. "The one with the fair hair!"

Lord Carrigan had the good grace to look disconcerted. "Here," he said, taking her arm, "let us go out onto the terrace. It is next to impossible to hear, now that the music is starting up."

And, indeed, the fiddles were making a loud business of it. There was no need to talk to him for more than a few minutes, Emily told herself. Besides, the air outside was refreshing, scented as it was by the flowers that were growing in great stone pots. Granted that there was little light except for what the moon provided, but there were other couples about and she did not feel that she would compromise herself.

"Let me begin by making an apology for David," Lord Carrigan began, leaning against a column. "You are quite right, Miss Brooke. He is my brother. And it is on his ac-account that I have returned from the Continent."

"He has been involved in escapades?" Emily asked him. "That seemed to be what Sir Adrian was implying."

"Escapade upon escapade," the gentleman beside her said in a low voice. "I had hoped that when our father died, he would take over the management of the estate in Sussex. But he is over twenty-one, and he prefers to run with the bucks in London. But that is my problem, Miss Brooke, and not yours. You will, perhaps, excuse me if I ask you what sort of difficulty you found yourself in which necessitated escape from Sir Adrian. Granted that he is something of a fool, but there are plenty of them about."

"I see you do not care for Society, sir," Emily replied.

"And I see that you avoid the question," he told her. "No matter. I only thought to have been of some assistance."

It occurred to Emily that she owed him some sort of explanation and that, indeed, she could make use of some advice. It had been a relatively simple matter to avoid Sir Adrian's attentions this time, but in the event he was persistent, she did not know what she could do. Clearly, this gentleman was sensible, and certainly he knew the ways of Society better than she. And so, because she had nowhere else to turn, she decided to confide in him.

"I have recently come up to London, sir, to join my aunt and cousins," she began hesitantly. "My aunt is Lady Fairfield. Perhaps you know her."

"Indeed I do," Lord Carrigan said dryly. "I met her once in Paris. Lady Fairfield is a very unusual woman, if you will allow me to say so. Admirable, but unusual."

"She is so singularly optimistic," Emily admitted. "Cheerful almost to a fault. Not that I mean to criticize my aunt, sir, but she makes herself so very vulnerable that she is often taken advantage of. Not the least by her servants. But that is by the by."

The moon moved beneath a cloud, and for a moment they were in perfect darkness. Emily began to wonder if she had been wise. Certainly this gentleman must find it singular that she should make a confidant of a stranger, even though he had offered to be one.

"I—I think that I have said enough and more," she went on, just as the moon appeared again, illuminating Lord Carrigan's handsome face. She had been afraid that she would find him smiling, but instead he wore an expression of concern.

"On the contrary," he told her in a low voice, " 'vulnerable' is the word that I would have chosen if you had asked me to describe your aunt. Her son is quite a different matter, I believe. He is a friend of my brother's and, from what I hear, he fancies himself a man-about-town."

The moonlight blazed on Emily's gown, turning the

white taffeta to silver. She knew that Lord Carrigan must see the worried expression in her eyes.

"My cousin gambles and carouses, and his mother thinks that he is the finest young gentleman in London," she continued. "If he continues as he is, her eyes must be opened sometime, and I dread to think how much she will be hurt."

"What of her daughter?" Lord Carrigan asked her. "I remember her as being a plump, jolly girl, who is as cheerful as her mother."

That was such a precise description of Phoebe that Emily could not withhold agreement. "She fancies Sir Adrian," she said.

"Which says a great deal for her lack of discrimination."

"Yes. That is it precisely. I only met him for the first time this evening, but I cannot think he is worthy of her, aside from being twice her age. She was so glad to see him and was quite certain that he meant to ask her to dance."

"And you, on the other hand, detected certain signs that he had designs on you instead," Lord Carrigan suggested.

Just as she had guessed; he was astute. Emily could only hope he could be trusted to keep a confidence.

"And so you made your escape and, when he followed, you called on me for assistance," Lord Carrigan continued. "If you care for my opinion, Miss Brooke, you have acted admirably, although perhaps not wisely, considering you have your cousin's happiness in mind."

Emily stared at him, bewildered. "I am afraid, sir," she murmured, "that I do not understand what you mean precisely. All of which is the root of my problem, no doubt, in that I do not understand London ways."

"It is a pity that you should ever have to learn them," Lord Carrigan said grimly. "What I meant was that, although it might have caused your cousin present unhappiness, it could have been for the best had you encouraged Sir Adrian."

"Encouraged him, sir!"

"Precisely. Then your cousin would have seen him for the gadabout he is. No doubt, it would cause her pain to be disillusioned, but in the end it would be best for her not to pin her hopes on the fellow."

A couple wandered past them, and the lady paused to smell the flowers in an urn close by. Emily waited until the two had strolled away before she made reply.

"Are you suggesting that I play some sort of elaborate game, sir?" she asked him. "Manipulate and rearrange other people's lives?"

"I assure you that it is the most popular game in London," Lord Carrigan said dryly. "Many people dedicate a lifetime to it. You, at least, would have the excuse of a good cause."

"But Phoebe would think I had betrayed her."

"She will meet betrayal so often that it is just as well she learn to recognize it."

"You are a great cynic, sir."

"It is impossible to survive in London in any other condition," he told her. "You may not like the advice I am giving you, but it is practical."

Emily took two steps away from him. "Are you saying that I must either choose to be like my aunt or become some—some sort of moral monster?" she demanded. "I thank you for your recommendations, sir. I see now that I should not have imposed on you. You have given me a deal to think about. And now, sir, good night."

CHAPTER FOUR

Emily scarcely knew where she was going when she hurried away from Lord Carrigan. She only knew that she did not want to go back to the ballroom and have to be taunted by those despicable young men or have to ward off Sir Adrian's advances. It was all very well for Lord Carrigan to suggest that things might go better if she were cynical. But the truth was, she could not bear to be responsible for hurting Phoebe, even though, in the end, it might prove the better thing.

A long, carpeted corridor, lined with rooms on one side and windows on the other, formed a sort of gallery just to the right of the ballroom, and it was here that Emily took refuge. Solitary candles in gold stands, which were set on small mahogany tables lining the wall, threw golden flares of light upward to illuminate the portraits of her hostess's ancestors. One painted gentleman, wearing a ruff, seemed to be looking at her in such an accusing way that Emily felt distinctly uncomfortable. What excuse could she give if someone were to come upon her in this part of the house? Would it be sufficient, she wondered, to plead a megrim and say she needed quiet?

That was partly true at any rate, she told herself, as she hesitated between two closed doors, wondering if she dared to open either. Her head might not be aching, but she badly needed to be by herself. Never for one moment had she thought that her first London ball would bring her so many problems. When she remembered the way Lord Carrigan's younger brother and his friends had circled round her and demanded a kiss, she felt a renewed surge of humiliation. And, when she thought of Sir Adrian and his cloying ways, she wanted to throw something.

Thinking that she heard someone coming, Emily made her decision and opened the door just to her left. At once she found herself in a library, the walls of which, except for two small windows, were completely lined with books. Indeed, the very air was thick with the rich smell of them. There was no light, except that which was thrown from a smoldering fire in the grate, but that was sufficient, not only to illuminate the books that stretched up into the shadows, but the heavy Chippendale furniture that crowded the room—deep armchairs with claw-shaped feet, a mahogany writing table with a lifted writing slope, and a ribband-back settee of an unusual design. The walls of the house must be very thick indeed, Emily realized, for she could hear no sound at all of the ball. With a sigh of relief, she dropped on the settee and stared into the dying fire.

Minutes passed before she became aware that someone else was in the room. It was the cough that alerted her, a cough that seemed to come from the very depths of one of the deep armchairs. With a little cry, Emily sprang to her feet. She had been luxuriating in a feeling that, for the moment, she was safe. Indeed, she had been relishing the thought that for the next few hours she could think about what had happened and make some plans about how she intended to conduct herself in a society that was quite unlike the haut monde she had expected. And now, to find that she had company! Perhaps even the master of the house, although she had assumed her hostess, Lady Courtiney, was a widow. But it could be that there *was* a husband who did not care for soirees, someone who would be outraged at such an intrusion . . .

"Pray excuse me!" Emily exclaimed, to be on the safe side. At the same time, she hurried toward the door, a little frightened. Certainly she knew that no one dangerous lurked in that armchair. Still, things and people that one could not see were always disorienting, at best.

"Don't hurry away, gel!" a crusty voice called after her. "Come back here and let me get a look at you! There's no good expecting me to stand up, because my bones are not all that good at bending now. What I am doing here, I do not know, except that Lady Courtiney was damned persistent. Can't think what she wants with an old fellow like me, can you? Eh?"

All the time that he was speaking, Emily had been hesitantly returning to the center of the room. Now she was close enough to both the chair and to the fire to see the wizened features of a gentleman who sat framed by the rich brocade of the chair. "Well, gel, I won't bite you," he declared. "My name is Lord Harmond, and who are you?"

Emily gave him her name, silently weighing what she should do. If he wanted her to leave the library, of course she would do so—if for no other reason than respect for his great age. But, even though he appeared to be singularly outspoken, she hoped that he would invite her to stay. In her mind's eye, she could still see Sir Adrian approaching her, and her imagination painted all too clearly the dawning recognition that would come to Phoebe's face.

"Well, Miss Emily Brooke," Lord Harmond declared, thumping his cane on the floor, in what might have been an attempt at a hearty manner, "what are you doing hiding away in a library? That's not the way of things for pretty girls at a ball. At least, if they hide away, they do not do so alone."

And, with that, he gave her such a sidelong glance as to suggest any number of improprieties. He was, Emily decided, a wicked-looking old man, with his old-fashioned white wig with rolled sausage curls at the side and a queue behind. His embroidered coat was very long and out of fashion, and the lace at his throat and wrist seemed yellow with age, although that might have been her fancy.

"I—I found that I had a megrim," Emily told him, "and came here looking for a quiet place."

"A megrim, eh!" Lord Harmond shouted in a tone of disbelief. "How you ladies do trot your headaches out for every occasion. Always have done and always will do. Well, my girl, I want the truth. Come now. It will do you no harm to give an old man a bit of diversion, 'pon my soul, it won't! Have you been jilted? Is that the way of it? No, you are too beautiful for that, I think. Either that, or your young gentleman has no eyes in his head."

"I have no young gentleman!" Emily told him, stung by the assumption that the only thing that might have distressed her would be someone of the opposite sex. And then, recollecting that was, in fact, the case, she felt herself begin to blush.

"I expect you have not met anyone you fancy," Lord Harmond said complacently. "Oh, you will be able to pick and choose, my dear. I was a bit of a gadabout in my youth and know about such things. Yes, yes. A gadabout. Although you would not think it to see me now."

Emily was quite prepared to believe him. Old he might be, but there was a sparkle in his eyes that age had not put out. Indeed, she quite liked him. And felt sorry, too. It must be sad to find that balls, like this one, wearied you and that you must steal off for forty winks in a quiet corner. Although Lord Harmond had not admitted to that, it was what Emily was certain he had been doing.

"This is my first London ball, sir," she said, sitting down on the footstool by his feet. "And, I confess, it has not been quite what I had expected."

"In other words, it has been a disappointment," Lord Harmond muttered. "Ah, well, that is the way of the world, my girl. It is never precisely what we expect. But I made it a point, years ago, to be the eternal optimist. As a consequence, I take substantial risks, you see. Ah, yes! Scarcely a day passes . . ."

The sentence ended with a little snore, and then he jerked himself awake and pretended to have sneezed. Watching him pull a handkerchief from the inner pocket of his coattail, Emily wondered what sort of risks he could possibly take and decided that he was just having his little boast.

"An old man must have his little crochets," her father had told her once. "There is little enough left to him, you will agree."

As a consequence, she only remarked that she hoped he was not about to take a cold and, at his urging, became a bit more precise about what had upset her.

"Well, in the matter of this fellow who your cousin has her eyes on," Lord Harmond muttered when she had finished, "he does not sound to me like a prize package."

Emily had told him more than she had meant to because of his kind manner, but now she held her breath, afraid that, like Lord Carrigan, the old man might recommend that she allow Sir Adrian to show his true colors and thus put Phoebe off him once and for all. But, instead, he asked her a simple question.

"How do you propose to handle the matter, gel? Damme, you may hide away from the gentleman this evening, but there will be other soirees. You cannot spend the entire time of your coming-out hiding away from him in libraries. Or, to put it differently, you *can*, but I would not recommend it."

Emily knotted her hands under her chin and stared into the embers of the fire, not seeing the smile that came to the old man's lips as he surveyed her lovely profile from the cavern of his chair. It was the smile of someone who admires beauty above all things, but Emily was not to know. Instead, quite preoccupied, she grappled with the problem.

"I can be honest with Sir Adrian," she said finally. "That is always best, I think. Tell him that I do not intend to encourage his advances and that it displeases me that he puts me in position to hurt my cousin. But no! I cannot say that! He does not know, you see, of her affection for him. To say anything of the sort I have just proposed might be to put him off her forever. At least, I have heard that gentlemen do not like to be pursued."

The old man cackled. "I have heard that old saw, too," he told her. "Damme, gel, it depends on who is doing the pursuing. Is your cousin attractive? Tell me that and you have told me all."

"Why, of course she is attractive," Emily replied, turning to stare at him. "Phoebe has very pretty ways. I mean to say that she is always cheerful."

"Why, then, of course, she must be a fool."

"Why, that is not the case at all, sir!" Emily cried, leaping to her feet. "She is simply like her mother as far as disposition is concerned."

Again the old man cackled. " 'Pon my soul, you have spirit, my dear. Tell me, you called her Phoebe. You would not be speaking of Miss Phoebe Fairfield, would you?"

Emily admitted that she was and promised herself silently that, if Lord Harmond continued to insult her cousin, she would leave him.

"Well, then, I have heard of her and of her mother," the old man said, making another feeble clatter with his cane. "I must say that I like their spirit. It is something to fly in the face of reality. I take my risks for much the same reason. That is to say, I do not care to admit that I am a victim of whatever powers there be. As a consequence, I set my own path, go in my own direction. Yes, yes! That is the great thing! Why, I declare, this conversation has quite set me up! The moment that I heard your name, I thought it might. Damme, you're like your father . . ."

A snore followed, despite Lord Harmond's claim that he had been "set up." It gave Emily some consolation to know that she had, apparently, been talking to a friend of her father's. But then it came to her that, after all the talk, her problem had not been solved.

CHAPTER FIVE

"Such a delightful party!" Lady Fairfield crooned happily the next morning as they sat together in the charming morning room over breakfast. "Don't you agree, Phoebe?"

"Oh, yes, Mama!" her daughter replied, cutting into a moist, warm scone with an expression of anticipation. Both her aunt and her cousin relished food as one of the many good things in life, Emily had discovered, and mealtimes for them were occasions of an almost religious celebration. As for herself, however, such a profusion of dishes as the sideboard offered had the effect of causing her to lose her appetite completely. Trying not to look at the roast of beef, the side of ham, the kippers, and the steaming mush cake topped with honey, she helped herself to a thin slice of bread and allowed her aunt to pour her a cup of tea from the silver pot that glittered in the morning sunlight.

"We could not think where you had gotten to last night, my dear," Lady Fairfield said. "But, of course, I did not worry, particularly since Sir Adrian told us that you were in such prestigious company."

Emily took her seat at the oak table and sniffed the roses in the vase appreciatively. Last night, on the return home, she had allowed her aunt to believe that she had, indeed, been with Lord Carrigan all evening, and that it was only because it was so crowded that she had not been seen. But, during a restless night, it had come to her that that was tantamount to a lie, and she had determined to be more honest in the morning. But, before she could speak, Phoebe had made an interruption.

"Why is Lord Carrigan so important, Mama?" she

34

asked, spreading the remainder of her scone with thick raspberry jam and topping that with butter. "Sir Adrian told me that he is very rich and that he is a marquess. Perhaps that is what you mean."

Lady Fairfield shook her head. For the mornings, she chose to wear a red and yellow dressing gown, which made her look like a whole field of poppies, while her faded red hair was covered by a voluminous mobcap tied about with an orange ribbon.

"I mean that he is such a well-thought-of gentleman," she said with a broad smile. "He is extremely handsome, of course, but there is no need for me to tell you that, my dear. He has a younger brother who is a friend of Jeremy's. A rather wild young man, I think, but I always say that gentlemen must sow their wild oats sometime, and it is better for it to be sooner done than later. But we were speaking of Lord Carrigan. His maiden speech in the House of Lords was very well received, I believe. I read about it in the *Gazette*. Of course, he is inclined to keep to himself and does not care much for Society, but that is *his* choice, after all. Would you like another scone, Phoebe?"

Emily did not want to be intrigued and yet she found she was. The night before, she had left Lord Carrigan because he had given her such dark advice. Indeed, he could not have disclosed himself as any more the cynic than he had. That was why it surprised her to hear her aunt speak of him in such glowing terms. Perhaps he hid his darker side successfully.

"You must ask Sir Adrian, if you want to know any more about Lord Carrigan, my dear," her aunt said, polishing an apple with her napkin. "Sir Adrian knows everything about everyone. But, as for me, I know little enough about Lord Carrigan at first hand."

"He said he met you once in Paris," Emily murmured, sipping her tea. It was absurd of her to have such an intense interest in the gentleman, she knew. He had been kind to her. Nothing more. And he had offered her advice of the sort she could not take. Doubtless, he had already forgotten her, or, if she were remembered, it was with annoyance to think that he had wasted his time with a silly girl who had been so gauche as to run away from him.

"Remember, Mama?" Phoebe was saying. "It was at

Madam Ferbarge's salon. You were talking about Saint-Cloud and how much you admired the view, and Lord Carrigan replied that doubtless that part of the city was picturesque, but that he could not bring himself to find even an uncertain charm in any place that housed so much poverty."

Lady Fairfield suddenly became quite discomposed, and, for the first time since she had arrived in London, Emily saw her frown.

"I understand he thinks a great deal of reform," she murmured, pushing her plate away. "And, of course, that is all very well. Everyone is not as comfortable as we are. I am quite aware of that. I give to charity. And I believe that I am generous."

"To a fault, Mama!" Phoebe cried. "To a fault!"

"Oh, dear," Lady Fairfield said with a smile that had something strained about it. "How did we stumble on such a serious conversation? I declare I cannot remember. And all because you had the great good fortune to spend the evening with such a charming gentleman, my dear."

"Sir Adrian *was* most attentive, Mama," Phoebe replied contentedly, taking another scone. "La! I see by your expression that you were speaking to Emily."

"*Both* of you were attended by charming gentlemen!" Lady Fairfield cried. "What could be better than that?"

It was time for Emily to speak, but before she could, Phoebe announced that she had never known until the evening before that Sir Adrian had such a grave concern for everybody's welfare.

"Why, he spent no end of time looking about for you," she said to Emily, wiping a little butter off her downy upper lip. "That was because he thought that Mama and I would be anxious. I declare, I think we must have looked in every room in the house, but we always seemed to miss you somehow."

"No one could be more thoughtful than dear Sir Adrian!" Lady Fairfield declared with great enthusiasm. "Even when I told him that I was certain you were quite safe as long as you were with Lord Carrigan, he would insist on looking for you, and when you did not appear for supper, he was quite beside himself. I told him there was certain to be an exclamation, but that, Lord Carrigan being absent, too, it had to be assumed that you were still together. So charming, I think, when two young people strike it off at their first meeting. I expect you talked and talked."

Emily was afraid that, given the opportunity, her aunt would create a complicated romance of which it might well be difficult to disillusion her. And so, before she could continue to build castles in the sky, the girl pushed back her chair and rose, by way of interruption.

"I *was* with Lord Carrigan at the beginning," she said. "We—we talked for a few minutes on the terrace. But, after that—after that, I found I had a megrim. There was no need to bother you or Phoebe, Aunt. I only needed to be quiet. And so I went into the library."

"Alone?" her aunt exclaimed. "You spent the evening in the library alone?"

"There—there was an old gentleman there," Emily told them, deciding that there was no harm in telling the whole truth. "We talked about this and that for a little, and then he took a nap."

"Well, then! Only fancy that!" her aunt declared. "At least you had some company!"

"It was a silly thing for me to do, no doubt," Emily murmured. "But . . ."

"On the contrary, my dear," Lady Fairfield declared, rising to come around the table, billowing in her red and yellow dressing gown like some exotic butterfly, "it was very generous of you not to want to spoil your cousin's good time. Here. Give me a kiss. What a good, dear gel you are to think of our enjoyment first. But you must promise me that if it ever happens again—if you so much as feel out of spirits—you will let me know."

The irony was, Emily told herself, that it did not seem a pity to deceive them about the megrim. Indeed, they were so gullible that, for some people at least, it must appear irresistible to take advantage. And yet, she had succeeded in telling only one untruth. And she *might* have had a megrim easily enough. At least, now, they would not assume an acquaintance with Lord Carrigan that she had no right to claim.

"Sir Adrian would have been much distressed if he had known that you were not feeling quite the thing," Phoebe assured her, as she, too, bounced up from her chair and

wrapped her cousin in a hearty embrace. "I am so glad he
likes you."

Such naiveté on Phoebe's part made Emily feel the full
weight of her responsibility. If Sir Adrian behaved in the
same way the next time they met—and she must prepare
herself for that eventuality, fond as Phoebe appeared to
be of him—she must find a way to rebuff him that would
not put him at odds with the entire family.

No sooner had she made this determination, all the
while returning her cousin's embrace and her aunt's fond
kisses, than the door of the breakfast room opened and
Jeremy put in a belated appearance.

The reason for the late hour of his arrival was apparent
to Emily, at least, at a single glance. Never had she seen
anyone more clearly suffering from having drunk deeply
the night before. His eyes were red and swollen, and his
complexion had turned a pasty white with faint tinges of
green. His walk was unsteady, and he seemed to suffer
from an inability to keep from clutching his head with
both hands as though he would like to wrench it off. Going straight to the mahogany buffet, he took the silver
pitcher of water and a glass and proceeded to drink glass
after glass of it, declaring between gulps that he was
dammed if he had ever been so parched, whereupon
Lady Fairfield beamed her approval and declared that, in
her experience, there was no more healthful drink than
water.

This remark caused Jeremy to clutch his head with a
sort of fury and beg his mother not to speak so loudly,
since he was afraid that his head would split. Instantly,
his mother was all concern and bustled off with Phoebe in
her wake to find various drugs and remedies that would
set him straight. As soon as she had gone, Jeremy called
for a raw egg and, having consumed the same with gri-
maces galore, addressed himself to Emily.

"Those damned females will be the death of me," he
said.

There was no need for him to indicate further who he
meant, although he rolled his eyes upward to the floor
above, where faint sounds of rummaging could be heard
together with the noise of banging drawers.

"I should think the claret might claim your life first,"
Emily said calmly. "The bottle takes a yearly toll, I un-

derstand, and just at present you look very like a candidate for a complaint of the liver."

Jeremy looked at her sideways and then full-faced, turning his head carefully as though everything inside might fall to rattling together if he did not have a care.

"You are not as gullible as they," he observed in a doleful voice. "I suppose you intend to tell them that last night I was in my cups."

"They think you such a fine chap that I do not think that I will disillusion them," Emily replied. "Besides, you seem to be suffering quite adequately, as it is, for your misdoings."

For a moment Jeremy did not answer and then, with a look that resembled the expression in a gentleman's eyes when he takes careful aim with a fowling piece, he delivered his shot.

"Your name was being bandied about in my company last night," he said. "It seems you have managed to acquire something of a reputation, Cousin. Why, she is as demure as a peahen, I told them. But David declared himself to be quite smitten and went so far as to promise to make a duel with his own brother over you if necessary."

Emily leaped to her feet at that. It was the habit of the household for everyone to come to breakfast in dishabille, and even Jeremy wore a dressing gown over his lawn shirt and his pantaloons. Emily's regalia, consisting of a billowing, white muslin robe and a white cap pulled over her dark curls, tended to make her look even younger than she was. But there was nothing of the child about her as she faced her cousin with blazing eyes.

"David!" she exclaimed. "I know no David! There is no need for you to make up lies, Cousin, simply because you are suffering from having had too much to drink!"

Jeremy clearly was not pleased at her directness. "Plain speaking demands plain speaking in return," he muttered. "You have not forgotten the gentleman you dallied with on the terrace last night, I hope. Afterward, when the two of you disappeared, David was quite nearly wild. Of course, port always inflames him, but I believe him when he declares to having developed a passion for you at first sight."

Emily drew her breath and held it. She remembered

now, only too well. Lord Carrigan had told her that one of the youths who had made a circle around her was his brother. The one who had demanded a kiss. He had said that the boy was wild and always up to escapades. And now, to find that he was one of the fine friends her aunt claimed for her son!

"I dallied with no one!" she exclaimed. "Oh, bother your head! I will speak in as loud a tone as I find necessary to impress on you that nothing could interest me less that what either you or your friends say."

Jeremy tried to manage a grin of conciliation. "No need to fly into the boughs," he said. "Dash it, I only meant to rag you a bit, Cousin."

"I find nothing to amuse me in anything you say," Emily assured him. "And if you talk this way before your mother, you will succeed in upsetting her quite unnecessarily on my account."

Jeremy eyed the kippers with distaste. "Damme, nothing can upset Mama," he said in an offhanded way. "You know what she and Phoebe are. Incurable optimists, both of them."

"Someday you will go too far," Emily warned him, starting for the door. "And when they see you in your true colors, it will be a dreadful shock of the sort they do not deserve."

With that, she whirled out into the hall in time to see an extraordinary-looking lady make an entrance at the front door.

"My dear man," this singular personage cried as the butler Danvers surveyed her with alarm. "Be good enough to inform your mistress that Lady Randolph has arrived. Then see to it that my portmanteau is brought in straightaway and a room prepared, for I have come to make a little visit."

CHAPTER SIX

Lady Randolph appeared to be quite accustomed to attracting stares. Indeed, she gave the distinct impression of being someone quite willing to attract attention in any way possible, no matter how rude and vulgar. Extremely tall and angular, she was of an age when many ladies begin to dress in plain greys and lavender and to wear their turbans very tight to disguise the changing color of their hair.

Clearly, this was not Lady Randolph's manner. On the morning when she arrived at the house on Cavendish Square, she was outfitted in a French-style chemise gown made of patterned muslin, which, since it was white, would have better suited a young girl. The bodice of the gown was cut very low, considering the lady's ample proportions, and she wore no fichu to disguise her charms. Otherwise, her appearance was decorous enough, for her arms were not exposed—no doubt with good reason. Indeed, the tight-fitting sleeves of her gown closed at her wrists with luxurious chiffon frills, which struck another girlish note.

But it was the lady's face that intrigued Emily as she and Lady Randolph stood staring at one another. The stranger's hair was a curious color that could not quite be called orange. It was cut very short and had been frizzed with an iron until it stood out from her head like a bush. Convention was re-established by the hat, which was a billow of white muslin with a lampshade brim, tied with a white satin ribbon underneath the chin, in just the way to hide any wrinkles that might be found there. And so color and style were assisted by dye, not to mention the paint

41

and powder that adorned her narrow face in an attempt to make maturity take on the characteristic flush of youth.

"Well, gel," Lady Randolph said in a sharp, mannered voice, well tinged with dryness, "when you are quite done staring, perhaps you will be good enough to show me to the drawing room. I am quite parched, I assure you. The coach from Dover jolted so, and the inns we passed were not the sorts of places where I would stop. I told the driver so. I told him, that at the very least, he should keep some bottled water on hand for passengers like myself who tend to be delicate."

Emily, who could only assume that her aunt had forgotten to tell her that she was expecting company, led the apparition into the very room she had expressed a desire to be in and watched her throw herself onto the settee. Irrelevant as it was, the thought struck her that the lady had made shift very well indeed, if she had traveled all the way up from Dover and had kept the white muslin of her gown in such perfect condition.

"I think that I must have a glass of ratafia," Lady Randolph said in her staccato voice. "Will you pull the bell rope, or shall I? Oh, I see there is a decanter handy! And a glass. Yes. Fill it to the brim, my dear. It will take more than one glass, I fear, to wash the dust of the Dover Road out of my throat."

And, taking the glass from Emily, she drained it in a single swallow. "Come here, my dear," she said, having so rapidly refreshed herself. "Sit down beside me. Oh, so you prefer to stand! I suppose you are dear Alicia's daughter. Dear me. When I met you in Paris, I can remember thinking of you as quite dowdy. What has happened to create this metamorphosis? Indeed, I cannot fancy that you are the same creature."

Emily was aware of a sense of something very like admiration for anyone capable of so much rudeness. Apparently, Lady Randolph had managed to assure herself that the world revolved for her benefit and that she had carte blanche to say anything she wanted to say. She wished to be considered young and so she dressed up like a girl and decided that the matter had been taken care of. She came whirling into someone's house, apparently quite unexpected, and behaved as though she were the mistress there. And now she took it upon her to make far from pleasant comments about the daughter of the house to her face, as she thought.

When Emily introduced herself, Lady Randolph did not appear to be taken aback. "I am glad to hear that you are not your cousin, Miss Brooke," she said with a brittle laugh. "Otherwise, I would have been forced to believe in miracles, something I prefer not to do. Surprises are so tiresome, I always think, and that is a consequence a miracle cannot avoid."

She said the words as though she were reciting lines in a play that was due to close. Beneath the thin surface of her vivacity, Emily thought she detected the flat surface of an awful boredom. She would be quite willing to believe that Lady Randolph was a perfect product of Society, flashy and superficial, witty and coy when need be, and frighteningly self-possessed.

"Up from the country for your coming-out, I expect," Her Ladyship said, her knowing eyes taking in every detail of Emily's attire. "Dear, dear! I shall have to take a hand with your gowns, I can see that now. What can your aunt be thinking of to let you dress in such an old-fashioned manner? Why, I declare, your sleeves are cut in last year's fashion, and no one is wearing an overskirt any longer. It is not *comme il faut*, as they say in Paris."

The impertinence of it took Emily's breath away, and her temper, which was always brought quickly to a boil, rose with disastrous speed. Whoever Lady Randolph was, and whatever her relationship to her aunt, she knew she did not like her. And it also seemed very clear that the lady would tread roughshod over anyone who did not put up a firm resistance.

"I am afraid my wardrobe will have to do, Madam," she said, making a frontal attack. "There is no money available for me to spend on clothes, but I assure you that it does not trouble me. Besides, coming from Paris as you apparently do, your eye is doubtless sharper than it needs to be in London. I do not know how long you have been away, but surely you recall that London ladies have a certain fondness for frumpiness."

"La!" Lady Randolph exclaimed, leaning back in the settee and raising one white-slippered foot in the air, in what, no doubt, she meant to be a girlish touch. The sunlight that darted through the long windows gave her orange curls a certain brassy quality that put the question of natural color to a severe test indeed. "La," Her Ladyship repeated, "you are a fiery little thing, aren't you? Temper! Temper! One of the first things a young lady should learn is never to waste a show. I mean to say, it does you no good to be angry with me. Gentlemen are the only people we should exercise our bad nature on. They take it to heart, you see, in a way women never do."

She walked the road closer to wit than Emily had imagined she could do, and it was clear from the look of self-congratulation on her bony face, that she was well aware of having nearly managed a bon mot.

"Another glass of ratafia, my dear!" she declared. "I declare I love the taste. But here is someone coming. Alicia! How delightful it is to see you! And this must be Phoebe. Why, you have become a beauty overnight! Such a charming dress. It suits you. Dear Alicia, I imagine you did not expect to see me quite so soon. But Paris is becoming something of a bore. The same people. The same conversation, and more than half of it in French, which is a perfect nuisance, as I am sure you will agree. I have just been having the most charming chat with your little niece here. A delightful child! Perfectly delightful! She was about to get me another glass of ratafia, but I expect she has forgotten."

Emily had forgotten for the excellent reason that it had become apparent to her, from the moment her aunt and Phoebe stepped inside the drawing room, that neither of them recognized their guest. And, judging from their unchanged expressions, nothing Lady Randolph had subsequently said had enlightened them as to her identity. A silence fell. The situation was manifestly clear. Emily observed that Lady Randolph seemed prepared for the eventuality, for, assuming a playful smile, she leaped to her feet, white muslin flying, and fell to embracing Lady Fairfield in the most familiar way imaginable.

"Why, my dear Alicia!" the stranger cried. "Don't tell me you have forgotten those delightful tête-à-têtes we had at the Duke d'Orléans's chateau! Or those enchanting picnics at the Bois! Why, we pledged lifelong devotion a score of times, and you insisted that I make your house my home the next time I returned to London!"

It was clear to Emily that her aunt was determined to

make the best of an awkward situation, for, as Lady Randolph released her, she assumed her customary smile, while Phoebe, ever constant in imitation of her mama did the same.

"La!" she declared. "I was only taken by surprise. Of course I have not forgotten . . ."

"Your dear Lilian," Lady Randolph prompted her.

"My dear Lilian," Lady Fairfield echoed her.

"You will recall that, when my husband Lord Randolph died and I was so distraught, you were the source of the greatest comfort to me."

"Yes, yes. Just so!" Lady Fairfield cried, doing her best to appear to recollect. "Poor Lord Randolph! Such a tragedy! I said so at the time. Do you remember, Phoebe?"

Her daughter bounced about in the excitement of attempted recollection. "Just so, Mama!" she exclaimed. "Just so!"

"Well, that is settled then," Lady Randolph declared, subsiding once again on the settee and closing her eyes as though in an excess of fatigue. "I was just telling your delightful niece that I am exhausted from my journey on the Dover Road. Indeed, I want for nothing more than some refreshment . . ."

She paused in such a pointed way that Emily had no choice but to resort once more to the decanter and pour another glass of ratafia.

"Yes," Lady Randolph continued. "Some refreshment and then a little rest. I hope I can be put in a bedchamber which faces west, for, while I cannot bear the sun in the morning, I dote on sunsets. You will remember how very fond I was of sunsets, Alicia. We often commented on it. I have such a passion for little things. Details. Not that I am particular on the broad scale. Quite certainly I will settle into your household routine with very little trouble. Why, all my friends will tell you that I am a perfect guest."

One of Lady Randolph's charms, it soon appeared, was that there was no need to assist her in the making of a conversation. Replies were assumed, and, if she wished to ask herself a question, she did so with very little reticence. It thus transpired that she had come to London for a lengthy stay, that her husband's brother, who had assumed the "title" at her husband's death was not "compatible," and that she was looking forward to helping "dear Phoebe" to enjoy a brilliant Season.

"I know any number of young gentlemen who will be grateful to me for introducing them to her," she said, hiding a yawn behind her fan. "And I will be pleased to help your niece to show herself to better advantage, Alicia, my dear. You know how generous I am. The poor child has pleaded poverty, you see, although I am certain that she exaggerates. But if, indeed, that is the case, I have any number of Paris gowns that can be overhauled to fit her. It is so fortunate that I have never lost my girlish figure. And now, my dear, I really must retire for a while. I do hope something is planned for tonight. You know how I dote on company, Alicia."

And, blowing kisses right and left, no doubt to demonstrate her generous nature, she drifted out of the drawing room in a haze of girlish muslin and dainty ways, leaving Lady Fairfield and Phoebe staring after her open-mouthed, but cheerful—or making the pretense.

Emily, who had held her tongue with considerable difficulty during Lady Randolph's performance, was the first to speak.

"You did not recognize her, Aunt," she said with accusation in her voice. "No matter what you said, you did not know her from Adam."

Lady Fairfield collapsed into a wing chair and shook her head in a dazed manner, still managing, however, to keep on smiling.

"But if she says that we were friends, my dear," she protested, "we must have been. Indeed, I think there was something very familiar about her. Don't you agree, Phoebe?"

"Oh, she was very familiar indeed," her daughter declared. "We must have known her very well from all that she was saying."

"Do you recall picnics at the Bois, Phoebe?"

"Not just at this very moment, Mama, but I am certain to think of them if I apply myself."

"And do you recollect ever being at the Duke D'Orléans's?"

"We went to so many houses, Mama, that it is no wonder that we cannot place it."

Emily allowed their duet to become a backdrop for her

own considerations. It was incredible to think of it, but it was her opinion that if Lady Randolph had ever met her aunt and cousin before, it had only been in passing. And, since it was clear that she was, to say the least, a worldly lady, it did not pass the bounds of imagination to think that, like so many other people, including the servants in this house, she had marked their naiveté in an instant and determined to take advantage of it when it might suit her.

Seeing that her aunt and cousin were still trying to prod their memories, Emily went to stare out of one of the long windows that faced the street, where Bert, the footman, and the groom were struggling with a portmanteau of considerable proportions. Clearly, Lady Randolph—if that was indeed her name—meant to make a stay of it, to take advantage of the hospitality of someone who did not even know who she was.

Turning back to face the drawing room, Emily wondered if she should tell her aunt and cousin what she thought. There was, she knew, little chance they would believe her, even in the face of such an excess of evidence to support her. But, this time, she could not sit by in silence.

She had just opened her mouth to begin, however, when Danvers appeared in the doorway, imposing, as always, in his butler-black garb.

"A gentleman to see the young master," he intoned through his nose, in a fashion that, he fancied, lent distinction. "The Right Honorable, the Viscount Carrigan."

CHAPTER SEVEN

Emily could only hope that she did not look as disconcerted as she felt. Her meeting with Lord Carrigan the evening before had left her, in a sense, bewildered. He had come to her assistance, and she had rewarded him by showing herself to be offended by his ideas. The suggestion he had made to her about Sir Adrian had certainly been practical enough. And he had not gone so far as to ask her to promise him that she would act on his advice. On the contrary, he had behaved precisely as a disinterested party should when approached by a stranger who insists on confiding her problems.

In that light, she could feel her cheeks grow warmer as she thought of what had happened. *She* had asked him to protect her from Sir Adrian's advances, and he had made no protest. She had explained the reason for her difficulties, and he had given her advice. And her thanks had been to leave him with an abruptness that would have better suited insult. And what crime had he committed other than to display a certain cynicism? And in that he had been quite right. Her aunt and cousin were prime examples of the way one will be taken advantage of unless one puts on armor. Lady Randolph was a case in point of the sort of person who will take extraordinary advantage given the opportunity.

Emily had been so busy with her thoughts that Lord Carrigan was in the room before she had decided on her attitude. And so it was that, while her aunt and cousin smiled and bobbed their heads and darted about indicating where everyone should sit and promising all the while

48

that Jeremy would be down directly, Emily remained where she was, by the window, and looked at him.

Inconsequential thoughts sped through her mind. Last night, at the soiree, she had thought that he would look his best in riding costume, and this morning she had proof of it. The jacket of bottle-blue superfine suited him precisely, as did the highly polished Hessian boots that glittered as he strode into the room. And he was even more handsome than she had remembered. But the most impressive thing was the air of competence about him, as though there was nothing he could not deal with. His life had order; Emily was certain of it. She thought of her father and the fatal fascination that he had for the Exchange. And then she thought of Mrs. Burbain and her kitchen purchases and of Danvers and the silver and now the added burden of Lady Randolph and she felt the full force of the dismay that had been building in her. How pleasant it must be to live a life in which there was a clear relationship between cause and consequence and no one dreamed idle dreams.

The moment to approach and join the group had clearly come, and Emily did so reluctantly, greeting Lord Carrigan with a murmur. Now that she looked at him directly, she saw that his face was grim. Surely a man-of-the-world, such as he, would not take the thoughtless snub delivered by a girl straight from the country so seriously. Not for a moment did she believe it, but all the same she was secretly embarrassed when she discovered how far from the fact that was for the reason for his visit.

"Jeremy will be with us at once, sir," Lady Fairfield said, when they had all settled in their chairs. "I believe that he was feeling under the weather this morning. Late hours do affect him so. He always had a delicate constitution, even as a child, and if he does not get nine hours' sleep—which, of course, he never does, being such a popular young gentleman . . . There now! I have forgotten the point I was making. But really, sir, this has been such an extraordinary morning. Still, everything is for the best. That is our motto, mine and Phoebe's, and, indeed, we are delighted at whatever circumstances have given us the pleasure of making your acquaintance."

It was a pretty, if incoherent speech, and Lady Fairfield delivered it with a smile that seemed to spring more genuinely to her lips than had been the case with Lady Randolph. As for Phoebe, she contented herself with bobbing her head in agreement.

"I am afraid that those will not be your sentiments as soon as I explain why I have come, Madam," the young Viscount said in a low voice. "But I think that it is only right that you should know. Indeed, I am surprised that you have had no news already, for I had half expected that the Bow Street Runners would already have been here."

"The Bow Street Runners!" Phoebe and her mother exclaimed in unison. And then both broke into merry laughter. "Lord Carrigan," Lady Fairfield exclaimed, "it is not fair to tease us. No doubt Emily told you we were credulous. Yes, dear! I know you think it and perhaps we deserve to be made cakes of."

Lord Carrigan glanced at Emily as though he understood a little better what she had hinted at last night. Rising, he went to stand beside the mantelpiece. "I assure you, Lady Fairfield," he said earnestly, "that I am not joking. I only wish I were."

"Has there been some tragedy, sir?" Emily demanded, conscious of a sudden sense of alarm. "Something serious has happened. I can tell it from your voice."

"Oh, surely not!" Lady Fairfield exclaimed and Phoebe echoed her. "You are too quick to anticipate disaster, Emily. But then, people cannot be blamed for their frame of mind, I expect. We all have our little ways."

Lord Carrigan's dark eyes did not stray from Emily's face. It was as though he had decided that they might as well be alone together and, no doubt, given his philosophy of life, they might.

"Is there any real need to distress my aunt and cousin, sir?" she murmured.

He hesitated. Emily could not think why her mind should dash off in tangents so. What did the fine lines of his lips matter? Of what consequence was it how his dark hair fell into a wave above his forehead? What a fool she was behaving! No doubt he would guess her thoughts and despise her accordingly.

"If they will be willing to speak to me openly and frankly," he said, "and Jeremy will join them in doing so, your household may be more fortunate than mine. Although I must confess I did not come here out of benevolence entirely, since there is some chance that Jeremy can be of assistance to my brother, if he will."

Although Emily was convinced that her aunt had not taken in more than half of what had just been said, she threw her a worried glance. Clearly, something was seriously wrong. The mention of Bow Street Runners would seem to indicate, in fact, that a crime had taken place. And the implication was that Jeremy might be involved.

"My son will be only too pleased to give you his assistance," Lady Fairfield declared happily. "He is *such* a one for thinking of other people! May I take it, sir, that your brother is in some slight pother or other? Young gentlemen, sir! Young gentlemen! But, then, you must know what I mean, for you are one of them yourself."

"Thanks to my brother's antics, I frequently feel older than my age," Lord Carrigan said dryly. "I would be happy enough if he had stuck to pother, as you call it, Madam. But this time, it appears he may have been guilty of a serious offense. And your son may be involved. There is no way I can or should keep you from knowing of that possibility."

"Nonsense, sir!" Lady Fairfield cried.

"Beyond belief!" Phoebe announced.

"Jeremy would never commit a breach of the peace!"

"My brother is certain not to be involved!"

"We shall laugh about this later on," Lady Fairfield announced, rising from her chair. "Come along, Phoebe. Let us find your brother and put him in a hurry. Poor Lord Carrigan is clearly much concerned, and the sooner that his mind is put to rest, the better."

Once the door was closed behind them, the young Viscount turned to Emily, who had risen when her aunt and cousin had left the room.

"Will you tell me just how serious it is?" she asked him. "You see how it is with them. They flee at the very hint of unpleasantness. I do not offer it as criticism, you understand, but it is how they are, and it sometimes makes them difficult to deal with. If you were to explain to me exactly what has gone wrong—"

"A friend of my brother's is missing," he said, before she could finish. "Young Robert Nicholson. He is a friend of Jeremy's, as well. No, hear me out. Last night the three of them were together, at the soiree that we attended and at other places besides. But Robert never returned home, and this morning his father, the Duke of Nicholson, claims to have received a note demanding ransom."

Emily drew a deep breath. "But surely," she began, "surely there is no suspicion—"

"That your cousin and my brother are involved, Miss Brooke? Is that what you are disclaiming? Because I am afraid that I must tell you—"

"I disclaim nothing!" Emily interrupted him, determined to make that point clear. "Do not confuse me with my aunt, sir! I only meant to ask a question—"

"And the answer to it is yes, Miss Brooke," the young Viscount told her. "No doubt you would have to know the Duke to understand how he could make such a charge. Some call him eccentric. Others say he is insane. In my opinion, he simply possesses an ungovernable temper and a conviction that his interests must be served before those of anyone else. In a word, he is impatient and he is proud. He has engaged Bow Street Runners in this business, and I do not presume to guess what else he might do."

"You—you have seen the Duke himself?"

"Unfortunately, yes. He took the liberty of coming to my house this morning to make his accusations. I have spent pleasanter half hours, I assure you. It was only with considerable difficulty that I persuaded him not to come here directly to repeat himself. From what you told me of your aunt last evening, I gathered that the shock of her encountering someone like the Duke without warning, of finding herself confronted with a man ready to hurl the worst sort of insult with absolute impunity, might easily be too much for her to bear."

Emily saw now what she had failed to note before: Lord Carrigan was clearly under a considerable strain. His face had a certain rigidness about it, and his dark eyes seemed to smolder.

"If Nicholson can gather the evidence he needs, he will have both your cousin and my brother up at Newgate," he continued in a low and bitter voice. "At least, that is what he claims."

Emily decided that she could serve the situation best by remaining as calm as he. And as much in earnest. They

could not have much time before they would be interrupted, and she determined that she would learn as much
before then as she could. And so she stood quite straight
and asked her questions—her face expressionless, a delicate but determined figure in her pale blue muslin gown.
It was not long before she had determined that Lord Carrigan's brother refused to say more than that he had been
in Nicholson's company, first at the ball, and then at
Ranelagh Gardens, where they had indulged in their usual
frolics. More than that he did not know or would not tell,
except that at one point, Nicholson had disappeared and
Jeremy with him.

"That is the primary reason I have come here, you
see," Lord Carrigan said in a low voice. While they had
talked together, they had, quite naturally, moved closer to
one another, until it had become necessary for Emily to
look up at him if she wished to see his face.

"To see if Jeremy can tell you where his friend is
now?"

"Yes. At least to give me a clue of some kind. The
Duke must be dealt with, you understand. Sometimes, I
think the man is mad. He treats his son abominably, you
know. But that is another story. Ah, here is your cousin
now."

Jeremy came into the room and shut the door firmly
behind him. His appearance had improved somewhat
since he and Emily had met at breakfast, but he was still
far from looking in the pink of health, and his mood
seemed to be one of deep despondency tinged with pique
at having been disturbed. The greeting that he exchanged
with Lord Carrigan was sullen at best, and when Emily
asked where his mother and sister were, he simply replied
that this was business for gentlemen and that she should
leave the room. Whereupon Lord Carrigan said, with a
sharp edge to his voice, that he would find it more agreeable to have her as a witness.

Although the morning was by now fairly advanced,
Jeremy was still in his dressing gown, and the fringes of
his lawn shirt, which were visible at the neck and wrists,
bore a certain crumpled quality, which hinted to Emily
that it might, indeed, have been slept in. This idea was
substantiated by the fact that Jeremy still wore his yellow
satin pantaloons, which had been his evening wear, al-

though he had discarded the red, high-heeled shoes in favor of calf slippers. These clues, joined to his condition when he had first come down the stairs, prepared her more or less for what he claimed, which was to the effect that he could remember having been with Nicholson at Ranelagh, but that about the time the third bottle of claret had been brought to the table, he had become a bit muddled about the sequence of events.

"To tell the truth, if you must have it," he muttered in conclusion, "I don't remember how it was that I got home. If David says that I went off with Nicholson, then that must be the way of it. But as for what happened to either of us after that, I have no recollection. In my opinion, Rob is up to some prank or other. Damme, he'll turn up like the bad penny that he is, take my word on it."

"I assure you, sir, that is what I would like to do," Lord Carrigan replied, slapping the riding crop, which he still carried, against his knee. "But I scarcely think that the situation can be remedied by aphorisms about bad pennies."

Jeremy assumed a careless air and let his dressing gown drag behind him as he sauntered the length of the room. "I am not likely to know or care what the Duke likes or dislikes," he declared. "I do not know the gentleman, and I do not intend to make his acquaintance now."

Until now, Emily had kept out of the discussion, but now she found she could contain herself no longer. Jeremy might have found a way to keep his mother and his sister from being present to state opinions, but she was on hand, and she must speak.

"If what Lord Carrigan says is true," she said, "it would seem that you may well have no choice about a meeting, Jeremy. If you were the last person seen to be with the Duke's son, then of course you will be questioned by the authorities, and doubtless by the Duke himself."

Jeremy shrugged his shoulders, although Emily suspected that his jauntiness was a pose. "Rob has told me enough about his father for me to know that he will not make a public scandal about family affairs. He may have employed the Bow Street Runners, but there will be no outcry of any sort. And now, if you will excuse me, I have other business."

And so he made an insouciant exit, leaving Lord Carrigan and Emily alone again.

"Perhaps," he said, "you can persuade your cousin to be more reasonable, Miss Brooke," he said. "It would be to his distinct advantage to be more open than he has been. At the very least, he might corroborate my brother's story."

"That is your primary concern, sir?"

"If you like to think so."

"And can you, perhaps, advise me of some trick or other by which I can get my cousin to confide or lie or somehow say what would be to your advantage?"

A few moments passed before he spoke. Dark eyes. Dark thoughts. Dark looks. "You are rapidly becoming a cynic, I see," he murmured. "A pity, that. But, of course, it could not be avoided, London being what it is. If your cousin's memory is somehow suddenly refreshed, perhaps you will let me know."

She watched him leave the room and, going to a window, watched him leave the house as well, a tall, handsome man, who swung onto his horse and rode away. And she was conscious of a growing bitterness. There were too many problems, none of them to be solved, it seemed, in an open way. And more than that, Lord Carrigan found nothing to approve of in the manner she faced the world. Not that his approval mattered, she told herself, tossing her dark curls. But, just in passing, she could not help remembering that at the ball the night before, he had been the one to suggest deceit as a means of dealing with Sir Adrian. And, today, he had implied that London was spoiling her.

"If nothing satisfies him, then I do not care," Emily announced to the empty drawing room. And it was only quite by accident that, in plumping up a pillow that she found on the settee, she somehow managed to fling it to the floor.

CHAPTER EIGHT

"My dears, the moment that I heard that Jeremy might be involved, I hurried over here to provide you with my advice and assistance. Tell me, has the Duke appeared as yet? Does Jeremy confess to anything? And is it true that David Carrigan disclaims all responsibility?"

Sir Adrian minced his way into the green salon, where Lady Fairfield and Phoebe had taken refuge, his quizzing-glass in one hand and a large, lacy handkerchief in the other. He was dressed in the pink of fashion, including a heavily embroidered waistcoat in greens and blues with two gold watches that hung from a gold chain across his chest.

Considering the fact that Emily had just broken the news to her aunt and cousin, they were bearing up very well indeed. Lady Fairfield was able to assume a feeble smile as she greeted her unexpected guest, and Phoebe went so far as to exclaim something to the effect that nothing could make her happier than to have such a dear friend on hand.

"I am certain that it is all a great mistake," Lady Fairfield said bravely. "The young gentleman will turn up safe and sound. I was just telling dear Emily that. We must always look on the bright side. Don't you agree, Sir Adrian?"

"That, Madam, is to assume there *is* a bright side," the gentleman replied. "Miss Brooke! I did not see you in the corner. Delightful! Quite delightful! And just think! Straight up from the country!"

This last he muttered, as though talking to himself, managing, at the same time, with a magician's flurry, to tuck his handkerchief away, take up her hand, and kiss it in the Continental mode. Glancing past him at Phoebe, Emily saw that her cousin's smile flickered and nearly died.

"I cannot think what the country should have to do with anything, Sir Adrian," she murmured, with such a degree of reproof in her voice as she thought might make him take warning. "London ways are at fault here, it seems. So much has gone awry that you will be doing us all a kindness if you would give advice."

And, with that, she joined her aunt and cousin by the fireplace and had the satisfaction of seeing Sir Adrian follow meekly.

"Tell me, do you think that I should worry?" Lady Fairfield began in what, for her, was a businesslike manner. "I have never done so in the past, you know, and I dislike making new beginnings. To put it another way, I have always found it just as easy to be content as to be dissatisfied, and yet, there have been times today when I have begun to wonder whether it is the better part of wisdom to persist. A lady I cannot recall having ever seen before has claimed me as an old friend and is presently a guest in this house. And now we have such curious news about a duke's disappearing son."

"What Mama wants to know," Phoebe interpreted, "is whether you believe that Jeremy is in any danger."

Sir Adrian took great care to separate and pull aside his coattails when he sat. "Your brother's first concern should be the Duke of Nicholson," he said, "the missing young man's father. The Duke is a monstrous fellow! Completely lacking in sensitivity. Boorish! Intolerant! Indeed, I consider him to be a perfect brute."

"Oh, dear! I'm sure he must be kind at heart," Lady Fairfield said hopefully. "Some people simply do not know how to present themselves to best effect."

Sir Adrian rolled his eyes ceilingward. "Dear lady!" he said. "You are determined to play the optimist to the end, I see. The facts are these. A gentleman is missing. Ransom demands have been made for his return. The two young gentlemen—of whom your son is one, Madam—who were last with him claim not to know what happened to him. The Duke, who is well known for having an uncontrollable temper, has decided to hold them responsible.

He had set Bow Street Runners asking questions about their character. And, although he claims he does not intend to make a public scandal, the fact is that half of London is probably as well informed as I am."

Phoebe bent a look of admiration on him. "Oh, but I think you do yourself an injustice there, Sir Adrian," she said. "Why I have heard it said that you are always the first on any scent of malicious gossip."

It was clear to Emily that Sir Adrian was disconcerted, although he must have known that Phoebe only sought to compliment him.

'Well, well!" he flustered. "That's as may be. But I have put the case before you as it stands, I think, and it is up to you to determine whether or not you should remain cheerful. I think you have already made up your mind not to do so, Miss Brooke. You will forgive me that I sense a certain irritation about you. London intrigues are always so exhausting, I think, and of course you have not built up a resilience to Society's ways as yet."

"You are quite right," Emily replied dryly. "I am rapidly becoming a cynic."

"Oh, you must never do that, my dear!" her aunt exclaimed. "I am certain that your Papa has confidence in me that I will not allow it. Besides, there are always two ways of looking at any issue. Sir Adrian has given us the worst, and I am prepared to give the best interpretation."

"Mama has thought it all out very cleverly," Phoebe declared admiringly, clasping her plump hands in her lap.

"Instead of being kidnapped, the Duke's son may have gone on a visit to the country," Lady Fairfield said in her most amiable manner. "Quite certainly he has friends there. Everyone has. He will send his father a message as soon as he arrives, and that will be an end to all of this dismal conjecture."

"But there is said to be a ransom note, Madam," Sir Adrian interposed.

"Idle rumor," Lady Fairfield proposed. "Or perhaps the Duke has simply misinterpreted an invitation. I know that I often do. You will remember, Phoebe, the time I took the note from Lady Clydesdale to be a bill from the milliner and . . ."

The disbelief in Sir Adrian's eyes in the face of her aunt's evasiveness would have amused Emily had the situation not seemed so serious. He opened his mouth to interrupt the plump little lady with the bulging brown eyes and then apparently changed his mind. As for Phoebe, she smiled delightedly as her mother continued to spin the story of the invitation she had mistaken for a bill.

"Now then," Lady Fairfield said comfortably when her tale was done and Phoebe had clapped her hands in silent applause, "you must agree, Sir Adrian, that what I have suggested makes it just as likely that the Duke of Nicholson's son has not really been kidnapped and that my son and another young gentleman are in no way involved."

"I pray that one story may be as nonsensical as the other, Madam," Sir Adrian replied in an awed voice. "Indeed, I find that now I am confused that—"

· He broke off as Danvers suddenly appeared inside the room. "Lord Nicholson," he announced in a doleful voice. "I would have asked for your permission to show him in, Your Ladyship, but he insisted otherwise."

Lady Fairfield and Phoebe leaped to their feet, and even Emily, taken by surprise, found that she was clutching the arm of her chair. As for Sir Adrian, he made little clucking sounds like an anxious rooster and aimed his quizzing-glass in the direction of the door.

Lord Nicholson made his entrance. He did not come into the room. Neither did he make an appearance. It was an "entrance" such as royalty might make, albeit without the flourishing of horns.

One look at the Duke was quite enough to assure Emily, at least, that he was no ordinary man. Tall and stout with a pugnacious face and beady, little eyes, he walked with his head thrust forward as though on the lookout for trouble. His frock coat was antiquated of cut, but made of the best superfine. Still, there was no air of elegance about him, but rather, an aura of repressed hostility, which told Emily at once why Lord Carrigan had seen fit to warn them about him.

"Lady Fairfield," the Duke announced, not troubling himself with the formality of introductions all around, "I shall want to speak to your son immediately. Eh, Rap! You here? No need to ask this lady if she knows what is going on then!"

Sir Adrian flushed and dropped his quizzing-glass and had to kneel to fetch it out from underneath the settee, all of which provided a distraction for Phoebe, but none whatever for her mother, whose brown eyes seemed quite likely to drop out of their sockets, although she gamely kept a cheerful smile on her lips.

"I am afraid, sir," she said, "that I do not know whether my son will see you, for he retired to his room not long ago and asked me expressly to see that he was not disturbed. I think, perhaps, he feels a bit under the weather."

"Damme, he was probably in his cups last night," Lord Nicholson exploded. "I've seen that rascal Carrigan, and he admitted to having been hornswoggled himself by the time they reached Ranelagh Gardens. I'll take that much as true, even if I don't think much of the remainder of his story. Your son will tell the same, I suppose. Well, well, it won't be long before those two young bucks will see that they have taken the wrong bull by the horns when they dared to challenge me!"

Having regained his quizzing-glass, Sir Adrian seemed to be torn between a desire to stay and an overwhelming need to go. As a consequence, he teetered and tottered back and forth on his tiny feet until Phoebe began to look at him quite anxiously. As for Emily, she had risen from her armchair and was staring at Lord Nicholson curiously, wondering if all the things that had been said about him were true and thinking it quite likely that they were. Meanwhile, her aunt maintained her smile.

"You are angry and upset, sir," Lady Fairfield declared, "and probably not without some reason."

"Some reason!" Lord Nicholson exploded. "My son has disappeared and been replaced by a ransom note, and you speak of some reason, Madam!"

He raised his fist and gave every appearance of being about to demolish the first item of furniture that came his way. Sir Adrian quavered visibly and blanched until he was the color of curdled milk.

"Would you care to have me remove the gentleman, Your Ladyship?" Danvers inquired in a casual sort of way. "I believe that Bert and I could manage between us if we tried."

Emily, who had not even noticed that the butler had remained in the room, still holding the knob of the open door, was startled. This was the servant who had, apparently, made off with her aunt's silver. And yet, he was loyal enough to offer her protection from the noxious behavior of someone so superior in rank to him as the Duke.

"Oh, that *is* good of you, Danvers!" Lady Fairfield cried. "To think of protecting me, that is. But I am certain that Lord Nicholson will control himself. I know what it is to worry about children, sir. That is to say, I have seen others do it, although I have never permitted it myself. Children are like weeds, I like to think. They do not need too much tending. Indeed, they often do best when left to themselves."

Lord Nicholson drew himself up until he looked like a rather large tree about to topple. "Do you mean to suggest, Madam," he shouted, turning purple as a plum, "that I am to allow my son to be kidnapped and do nothing? Nothing?"

"Let me tempt you to take a seat, sir," Lady Fairfield replied as though they had been exchanging pleasantries. "Danvers, see that the gentlemen are provided wine. There is some rather nice claret in the cellar, I believe."

"This is not a social call, Madam!" Lord Nicholson declared, and Emily, to her surprise, saw that he was somewhat mellowed. Or perhaps he was simply confused, since Phoebe had taken his left arm and Lady Fairfield his right and together they were guiding him to a chair.

"Perhaps it was not meant to be," her aunt declared. "But that does not mean it cannot become one. Nothing is ever so bad as it appears, sir. That is my philosophy."

"And a damned silly one, too," the Duke grumbled, allowing himself to be pushed and patted into a wing chair. "I confess to not being able to make you out, Madam. "What are you staring at, Rap? Surely I can take a seat if I've a mind to."

"Quite so! Quite so, sir!" Sir Adrian replied. "I never would have questioned it."

"Now that we are cozy," Lady Fairfield announced happily, "we can talk quite sensibly about this matter."

The Duke muttered something about not thinking *that* very likely, but he was unquestionably subdued. And when, just at that moment, Bert, the footman, appeared with a tray, he did not refuse the wine that was directly poured. Sir Adrian emptied his glass in a single swallow,

Emily noted, but the Duke appeared to savor his, much to Lady Fairfield's obvious delight.

"Has your son friends in the country, sir?" she asked.

"Eh? What's that? What's that?" Lord Nicholson exclaimed. "Friends in the country? Why, of course he has."

"Just as I thought," Lady Fairfield replied, smiling broadly. "That was precisely what I was saying not ten minutes ago. No doubt he has gone to visit them, sir, and you will return home to find a message waiting you to that effect."

"Madam," the Duke replied, "I am in possession of a ransom note. I have told you before and I will say it once again. My son has been kidnapped."

"Are you quite certain that it is not a bill?" Lady Fairfield inquired sweetly.

The Duke pulled a crumpled piece of paper from his waistcoat pocket and read from it in a penetrating voice, to the effect that if he wished to see his son again, he must be prepared to pay five hundred pounds.

Lady Fairfield remained unfazed. "Well, then," she said decidedly, "it must be a prank. Is your son a tease, sir? I know my own is. Or perhaps you and your son have quarreled and he wishes to give you a little scare."

"Quarreled!" Lord Nicholson exclaimed. "Why, we do nothing but quarrel and always have. You are suggesting that he sent this note himself, Madam? Ah, ha! I see it now! Your son has given you some information—"

"Jeremy has told me nothing," Lady Fairfield began. But, before she could continue, the door to the salon burst open, and Lady Randolph made her appearance in the most dramatic way. Her white muslin gown had been replaced by one of pink, cut in such a demure and somehow suggestive manner as to make her a rather shocking sight. Her orange curls had been decorated with ribbons, and the color of her cheeks was unnaturally high.

"Dear me!" she cried. "I did not mean to interrupt. I only thought—"

The Duke leaped to his feet as though he had suffered a sudden shock. "What is this woman doing here?" he bellowed. And then, louder still, "What sort of a household is this? I demand to know!"

CHAPTER NINE

Mr. Drew's legal chambers at the Inns of Court were musty and dusty and quite what Emily had imagined that they would be. Two clerks, one very young and the other very old, perched on high stools in the outer office and applied themselves to reading legal manuscripts by the illumination of the few beams of sunlight that made their way through the diamond-paned casement windows with a view over the Thames. A third clerk, whose skin was like parchment paper from lack of being in the open air, saw to it that she was comfortably seated in one of the straight-backed chairs that lined the wall facing the inner office, where, apparently, the solicitor had his private domain.

"Mr. Drew will not keep you waiting long," the third clerk explained. "The clients who are with him now should be on their way directly."

Emily indicated that she was quite willing to wait, and, indeed, she needed time to think. So much had happened in the space of a single morning that she had made her way here in the afternoon with only one thing steady in her mind, which was that she needed sensible advice.

At first, she had held out hope that her aunt would accompany her to Mr. Drew's legal offices, but Lady Fairfield had been obdurate in insisting that there was no real problem.

"Of course, it is very strange that the Duke and Lady Randolph should know one another," she had said, when quiet had finally descended on the house. "But then again, why should they not have made one another's acquaintance previously? After all, the ton is a closed Society. Everyone knows everyone else. I only meant that it was strange that the very sight of her should have thrown him into such a tantrum. I declare I could not make head or tail of what he was saying."

"I think that he was accusing her of somehow being responsible for his son's disappearance, Mama," Phoebe had suggested. "But, then, he is in a very suspicious mood."

"I do not think the poor man knew what he was saying at the last," Lady Fairfield had volunteered. "But, as for there being any cause to see Mr. Drew, Emily, I think you are making mountains out of molehills. Everything will resolve itself, if we stay calm. Besides, Phoebe and I are engaged to play at whist this afternoon, as usual, and I always think it best to keep to one's routine."

And with that, they had gone upstairs quite happily together to make their toilet, leaving Emily to consider what she should do next, which meant that she had been forced to review the awkward scene that had ensued when Lady Randolph had whirled into the room and caused the Duke to make his strange demand about the nature of the household.

"Why, Lady Randolph is my guest, sir," Lady Fairfield had told him cheerfully. "It appears that we were great, good friends in Paris sometime in the past, and she has been gracious enough to make us a visit now that she is in London."

That had seemed to Emily to be straightforward enough, given the circumstances, but the Duke of Nicholson had flown into a perfect fit, which rendered him nearly incoherent. The lady, he declared, was not what she had pretended to be or what she was still pretending, for either Lady Fairfield was being made a dupe or she was in complicity. From further ravings, it appeared to Emily that he favored conspiracy, and he would see that none of them got away with it, whatever *it* might be. He seemed to suffer from the notion that sometime in the past, Lady Randolph or "whatever she calls herself at present" had tried to compromise his son. There was some confused talk of the theatre and of the lady being on the stage.

"Why, all the world's a stage, sir," Lady Fairfield had said pleasantly, which remark had, for some reason, sent

His Lordship into a perfect passion, in the grips of which he barged his way out of the room, with Lady Fairfield and Phoebe in his wake, murmuring soothing suggestions, none of which he seemed to hear.

Left alone together, Sir Adrian and Emily had looked at Lady Randolph, and she had returned their gaze with a degree of innocence which would have better graced the face of a child of five. The silence growing awkward in the extreme, Emily had introduced Sir Adrian, who had then declared that he thought they must have met before, since Lady Randolph looked somehow familiar.

"I am afraid you are mistaken, sir," she had replied demurely. "I have been some time upon the Continent, you see."

This vagary had not appeared to satisfy Sir Adrian, who continued to survey her through his quizzing-glass as though she were a rare and curious object that must be more accurately identified.

"Perhaps," Emily had said, "you can explain why Lord Nicholson fell into such a rage on seeing you, Madam?"

But explaining either Lady Randolph could not or was not prepared to do. When pressed, in fact, she pouted like a girl and flounced about, finally taking her departure, in search, she said, of "Dear Alicia," with whom she must gossip a bit about old times.

"There is a mystery here," Lord Adrian announced when he and Emily were alone. "Dear Lady, you must confide in me. Whatever you say will go no further, I assure you."

Following which announcement, he had minced toward Emily in such a single-minded way that she had retreated from the green salon in time to see Lady Randolph and Jeremy in close discussion in the hall. It had been at that point that she had determined that Mr. Drew should be consulted, and when subsequently confronted by her aunt's refusal to accompany her on such an errand, she had taken matters entirely into her own hands.

Now, however, sitting in the solicitor's dingy outer office, Emily discovered that she was not precisely certain what she should say. And she was still wrestling with this problem, when the door before her opened and Mr. Drew himself appeared in the company of Lord Carrigan and the fair-haired young gentleman who had tried to kiss her at Lady Courtiney's ball.

"My dear Miss Brooke!" Mr. Drew exclaimed, peering at her through his spectacles. " 'Pon my soul, I did not know we had an appointment today."

Pretending to a composure she was far from feeling, Emily replied that she had come about a small matter of unexpected business and that she hoped he could spare her a few minutes of his time, all the time intensely aware of Lord Carrigan's dark-eyed attention to every word she was saying.

"You know His Lordship, I think," Mr. Drew said, after having offered her his assurance that she should have as long an interview as she liked. "I mean to say that I am aware that he has recently visited your aunt. And this is his brother, the Honorable David Carrigan. Perhaps you have not made his acquaintance."

"Why, as for that," the young man declared, making an exaggerated bow, "it is not for lack of trying on my part, if Miss Brooke does not know me very well indeed."

He appeared quite ready to continue in this teasing vein had not Lord Carrigan muttered something to him in a low voice, whereupon his brother indulged himself in another bow and declared that it seemed he had been ordered to wait in the street outside.

"My brother is in no mood to be argued with today, Miss Brooke," David Carrigan said as he departed. "But we will meet again. I declare I will make a point of it."

"I would ask you to excuse him," Lord Carrigan said when the young man was gone, "except that I can see no reason for you to do so, Miss Brooke. I wonder, Mr. Drew, if I could use your inner chamber for a moment to exchange a few private words with this lady. If, that is, she will permit it. The proceedings that we have just been discussing may, as a consequence, be facilitated."

To this suggestion the solicitor was so agreeable that Emily did not see how she could refuse. A moment later found her and Lord Carrigan alone in a musty, book-lined chamber, the atmosphere of which was singularly dank, despite the hissing of a small coal fire on the hearth.

Lord Carrigan threw his gauntlet gloves on a desk that was heaped with papers and offered Emily a chair, which she refused with a shake of her head. She was glad that she had chosen to wear a Windsor bonnet with a veil, for, somehow, she did not wish to meet his eyes directly. This gentleman had accused her of rapidly becoming a cynic when they had met earlier today, and the comment stung her still. What interpretation he would put on her visit to Mr. Drew, she did not care to think about.

"I will come directly to the point, Miss Brooke," he said. "It is an accident that we employ the same solicitor. My visit here was occasioned by the threats that Lord Nicholson has made against my brother. May I inquire if it is because of the Duke that you have come here? Has there been some new development since I left you this morning?"

Emily had not really expected that he would want to talk about anything but business. Still, she was strangely disappointed. Perhaps, at the back of her mind lurked the thought that he might have chosen this moment to be private with her in order to somehow soften the criticism he had made of her earlier in the day. What a fool she was to think that in this new world she had entered, there was any room for thoughtfulness! The first time they had met, he had counseled cynicism, and the second time they had been together, he had accused her of becoming worldly. Emily determined that, this time, she would give him no grounds for him to form any opinion of her at all. Hopefully, at any rate, it would be the last time they would ever meet.

"Lord Nicholson paid us a visit," she replied, keeping her voice expressionless. Since his brother and her cousin were in much the same boat, it would do no good to keep information from him. But she would make it clear that any communication between them was impersonal.

"I was afraid of that," Lord Carrigan said grimly. Clenching his hands behind his back, he stared into the fire. Outside, the sky must have grown cloudy, for it grew very dusky inside the book-lined room. Quite suddenly, Emily felt that everything that had happened, and was happening, had a dark, nightmare quality. She wanted to rebel against it, but she was captive in this room and in this city. All that she could do was to stand with her head high, a simple girl from the country, with her shabby pelisse and hand-embroidered reticule. At least, that must be how he saw her. How could he know how she raged inside?

"Were your aunt and cousin much upset?" the young Viscount demanded. "If Nicholson behaved as he did when he came to see my brother, it might have been a shock for them."

"My aunt was not particularly perturbed," Emily replied. "Nothing that the Duke could say convinced her that anything serious had happened."

For a moment he was silent, still staring at the burning coals. "And is that what you think, as well?" he asked her finally. "That it is nothing but some kind of prank, one that might involve your cousin and my brother. I don't think so, because otherwise you would not be here."

"You are assuming the nature of my business, sir," Emily replied.

It was a rebuff, and she saw his shoulders stiffen. What was there about this gentleman, she thought, that made her say what she had never intended?

"The fact is, sir, your observations are correct," she went on quickly. "The Duke has made certain accusations. My aunt will do nothing to defend herself or Jeremy. Other things are going on which I do not understand . . ."

He turned toward her. "Perhaps if you could confide in me," he said, "we might both benefit. I want nothing better than to get this matter finished and done with. At present, all that I really know is that Nicholson is making accusations right and left and claims to have a ransom note."

"He took it from his pocket and read it to us," Emily replied. "I did not actually see the words, but, unless the man is mad and has manufactured his own evidence, I must believe that the communication is what he says it is, the demand for his son's release being five hundred pounds."

"To be delivered under what conditions?"

"There was no mention of conditions. At least, not in what he read. I take it that he did not show you the note."

They were, she realized, talking quite intimately together. The words came naturally. There were no rough edges between them to cause scars. And he was right, of course. They could help one another. She decided that she would tell him the rest of it and let him see what he could make of the puzzle.

"We were distracted directly after he read the note," Emily began.

"By 'we' you mean . . ."

"My aunt and cousin Phoebe and Sir Adrian Rap."

Lord Carrigan scowled. "Rap there!" he grumbled. "The story will be all over town well before evening. But no matter. You said you were distracted from the ransom note."

Quickly, Emily informed him about the unexpected descent of Lady Randolph upon the household and confessed to her suspicion that not only could her aunt and cousin not remember her, but that they had, in fact, never known her before at all.

Lord Carrigan stared at her intently. The room had grown so dark that even though they stood close to one another, it was difficult to see the exact expression on his face.

"You mean to say an absolute stranger may be living in that house," he said in a low voice.

"She is not a stranger to everyone," Emily told him, her own voice falling to a murmur. "Lord Nicholson fell into a fury when he saw her. Indeed, he was incoherent, although I think he said something of her having been on the stage. And, in a general way, he accused her of complicity in his son's kidnapping. And that is not all."

"What else?" the young Marquess demanded, and Emily felt his hand on her arm. No doubt in the urgency of the moment, he did not realize what he was about. She did not draw away.

"I think that Jeremy knows her, too," Emily replied. "I saw them with their heads close together in the hall directly after Lord Nicholson left. And when they saw me watching them, they went into the library and shut the door."

Lord Carrigan's grip tightened on her arm. "I do not like the sound of it," he said. "Can you arrange a meeting between me and this Lady Randolph? I think you are right to be suspicious. I think, perhaps, that if we work together, we can put our finger on the truth. There is only one thing . . ."

"Yes," Emily replied. "What is it, sir?"

"You must be prepared to see something of the dark side of this little world," he said. "You are so very young. It is a pity to disillusion you."

"Perhaps," Emily told him, "I had fewer illusions than you thought, from the beginning. I do not mind much for myself, but my aunt has made a lifetime's work of thinking nothing but the best of everyone."

"Then we can only hope that her son is not involved in this so-called kidnapping," Lord Carrigan replied, taking his hand away from her arm quite suddenly, as though he had just realized that it had strayed there. "And my brother, as well. But the truth must come out, whatever it may be. And I think the first step we must take is to find out the truth about the mysterious Lady Randolph."

CHAPTER TEN

"To be absolutely frank, my dear," Lady Randolph declared, pausing where Emily had intercepted her on the stairs, "I do not care to act as chaperon for you and your young Lothario. And, although I am sure that you will claim otherwise, that is what you really want me to be."

"Lord Carrigan is not my Lothario!" Emily protested. "He is a casual acquaintance. A very charming man. And he has a wish to meet you."

Although it was the middle of the afternoon, Lady Randolph was now in dishabille, as though to indicate that her life was one long change of costume, and she had clearly been experimenting with her hair, which she had fluffed into a girlish, orange halo. Apparently, it was not necessary for her to exercise her charms when she was speaking to someone as unimportant as a fellow guest in the house, for her tone was sharp and her accents did not seem as delicate as they had been this morning. It was clear, as well, that she did not mean to linger to make idle chatter, for she put out her arm as though to brush Emily, who was standing just below her on the stairs, aside.

"Lord Carrigan will be disappointed," Emily said, searching her mind for a reason. "Since you know my cousin Jeremy, he thought that you might know his brother as well."

Lady Randolph made a rude sound at the back of her throat. "You must be mad!" she said. "Carrigan? Why, I have never heard the name."

"No doubt because you have been away so long on the Continent," Emily said quickly, taking her advantage.

71

She had not meant to say anything of the sort, but once the words had slipped out, she knew that they had struck home like a dart.

"You fancy yourself quite a wit, Miss Brooke," Lady Randolph said, spitting out the words. Now that she was angry, no amount of vermillion on her cheeks and lips, not to mention the dye in her hair, could disguise the fact that she was at least a score of years older than she pretended to be. "I do not know the name Carrigan. I do not wish to know anyone possessing it. Now, let me by!"

"Are you as friendly with Lord Carrigan's brother as you are with my Cousin Jeremy?" Emily inquired.

Lady Randolph could not disguise the fact that she had been taken by surprise. Her shifting eyes told Emily that she was deciding what course to take. It *had* meant something, then, that she had seen them in conference this morning. This woman was not quite a stranger, even though she was here on false pretenses. Lord Nicholson had recognized her. That must have given her some pause. And now she could not be certain just how much Emily knew that was not to her advantage.

Emily did not interrupt the silence that followed. The longer Lady Randolph thought, the more likely she was to take a less hostile stance. Whether she would see Lord Carrigan, of course, was still in doubt. But even if she did not, Emily knew something now that she had not known before.

Indeed, the afternoon had been full of surprises, from the moment she had met Lord Carrigan at her solicitor's chambers to the private discussion with the young Viscount, ending in their agreement to work together. And there had seemed nothing strange about Lord Carrigan's request that he join Mr. Drew and her in their discussion, since it was very likely his own earlier consultation had dealt with the degree of abuse that Lord Nicholson could be permitted to deliver without giving cause for legal action.

"I cannot imagine Aunt Alicia taking legal action against anyone," Emily had murmured, and Mr. Drew had declared that he agreed that it was most unlikely, but that it was still a useful thing to know.

"I do not intend to stand the same sort of harassment

he provided today," Lord Carrigan had said in an even voice. "And I shall tell him that myself if he presents himself at my house again."

"Unless, of course, he carries proof," Mr. Drew had said.

"Yes, there *is* that," the young Marquess had agreed. And he had still been frowning when, on reaching the street below, with Emily beside him, his brother David was observed to be shooting dice with a small group of street loungers, who could not, by any stretch of the imagination, be classified as gentlemen.

"Lend me five shillings, will you, Hugh," the young man demanded with a smile. "At least, when one games on the street like this, the wagers are not high. Damme, if I could not have lost five guineas at White's in exactly as much time as it took me to lose five shillings here. There's a lesson to be learned there somewhere, Miss Brooke. Perhaps if you discern what it is, you will let me know, for I am little good at drawing morals from life. My brother will agree to that, I know."

"I suspect that Miss Brooke has better things to do with her time, sir," Lord Carrigan remarked. And then, it being determined that Emily had come on her journey down the Strand in a hackney cab, he offered to drive her home in his phaeton, which was standing by the curb. Declaring that he was off to White's, his brother took his leave, and directly afterward Emily found herself being driven expertly down the crowded street.

"I should have warned you, perhaps," Lord Carrigan said as he flicked the reins, "that it is not the customary thing for a young lady to appear alone in public with a gentleman."

Emily tossed her head, thinking that she detected a challenge in what he said. "I have decided to obey the rules that are sensible and disregard those that are not," she told him. "The very fact that I visited Mr. Drew alone must have told you that."

They were, in fact, attracting some attention, particularly as they reached the vicinity of St. James's Park and the fashionable Mall. Three ladies leaned out of a lozenged coach, which was passing them, and there was an excited chatter.

"I think it is possible that you have not quite decided what posture to adopt," Lord Carrigan told her, turning the phaeton in the direction of Piccadilly so as to avoid both park and mall. "No doubt your natural impulses are warring with the practices that the ton imposes. I saw that at once, the first evening that we met, when I advised you how to deal with Sir Adrian's attentions. I went too far and shocked you, but I did not realize that you were so . . ."

"So innocent?" Emily demanded.

The crush of traffic had become so great that Lord Carrigan was forced to turn his full attention to his driving, but when he did respond, it was in such a serious tone that Emily was taken by surprise.

"There is nothing wrong with innocence," he told her, "but to practice it in the midst of so much unscrupulousness and hypocrisy is to take a certain risk. Your aunt and your Cousin Phoebe are a case in point, for, from what you tell me, they seem to be taken advantage of at every turn."

"At least they remain unconscious of it," Emily replied, "which is not to say that they are right. However, they remain cheerful."

"And let the world rage around them," Lord Carrigan mused. "Would you prefer to do the same?"

"I only know that the alternative does not present attractions," Emily murmured. "Sir Adrian thinks of nothing but scandal and is quite content to lead Phoebe on. Your brother and my cousin seem to live for nothing except pleasure. Lord Nicholson is so full of violent emotion and suspicion that he is scarcely sane. Lady Randolph, whoever she may really be, practices duplicity. It is as though London corrupts in one way or another. Why, even my father . . ."

She bit her lip and made a pause. Why was it that with this gentleman she always said more than she intended? No wonder he thought her innocent and, no doubt, despised her accordingly. She had not added him to her list, but she thought it probable that he was being kind, because he thought she might be of some assistance to him in regard to his brother.

Still, she was thankful to him that he did not press her

about her father. Instead, he turned the conversation to himself.

"If I am a cynic," he said in a low voice, "it is because it has been necessary. But I do not congratulate myself on reaching that exalted state, as you may suppose."

It was on that note that they reached the house on Cavendish Square, in time to see a butcher's boy driving a wagon heaped with packages down the alley that led to the courtyard behind the house. Seeing him, Emily gave an involuntary sigh, which caused Lord Carrigan to look so concerned that she gave him an explanation of Mrs. Burbain's purchasing practices for the kitchen.

To her surprise, the gentleman beside her burst into laughter. "It is so precisely what your aunt would allow to happen," he declared, drawing the phaeton to a halt before the front of the house. "But, still, if she can afford it . . ."

"She cannot afford it, sir," Emily retorted. "And yet there is nothing I can do, since she refuses to believe that it is happening and will not make a close examination of her accounts. Still, I am delighted to have amused you."

"Do not be angry with me, Miss Brooke," Lord Carrigan said, leaping to the ground and handing the reins of the horses to an urchin who stood ready before the great house for just such an opportunity to earn a penny. "Come, let me help you down. You remember your promise to introduce me to the mysterious Lady Randolph. From what you have told me, it is quite possible that she is somehow involved in this imbroglio concerning the Duke of Nicholson."

Reminded once again that the only thing between them was business at hand, Emily suppressed her irritation and, as soon as Danvers had shown the young Marquess into the drawing room, went in search of Lady Randolph, only to find her on the stairs.

All this she had time to remember as Her Ladyship considered Emily's suggestion that she was no stranger either to Jeremy or Lord Carrigan's brother.

"You are a peculiar gel," Lady Randolph said at last, examining her antagonist with narrowed eyes in a way that made her appear fully her age, despite the carrot-colored hair and the vermillion. "You pretend to be so demure, and yet, unless I am mistaken, you are attempting to blackmail me."

"I simply find it odd that you should have arrived without warning, Madam, and have insisted on an acquaintance with my aunt that clearly she cannot remember, even though she makes a pretense to," Emily retorted. "You make yourself as much at home in this house as though it were yours. The very sight of you is enough to drive Lord Nicholson into a state of singular distraction. And now you refuse to meet a friend to whom I would present you."

Lady Randolph scowled. "Oh, very well," she muttered. "If you insist. But I shall have to slip on a gown and make myself presentable. Just let me go upstairs . . ."

It occurred to Emily that if she let the lady out of her sight, she and Lord Carrigan might wait for her in vain.

"Since you did not bring an abigail," she said in a determined way, "you will, perhaps, allow me to assist you."

It was clear that this was not at all what Lady Randolph had in mind, but no doubt seeing that it would be awkward to refuse, she did not attempt to prevent Emily from following her to her bedchamber, which, although she had only been in the house a matter of hours, was strewn with clothing, the open portmanteau standing in the center of the room.

"If I had known that everything here would be in such a state of confusion," Lady Randolph declared, throwing off her dressing gown and groping under the bed for a petticoat, "I would have gone to one of my other friends."

"I thought you had been on the Continent so long that you had quite lost touch with everyone, Madam," Emily remarked dryly, meanwhile taking careful note of the fact that most of the gowns that were strewn about were of a far more sophisticated style than the white muslin frock that Lady Randolph had made her arrival in. She wondered why it had seemed necessary for Lady Randolph to adopt such a pose, but failed to come to a conclusion. There was no doubt a mystery here, which, for her aunt's sake at least, she would have to solve.

Meanwhile, Lady Randolph, with the assistance of the contents of the various pots and bottles on her dressing table, was making a girl of herself again. It was with a certain admiration that Emily observed how skillful she was in transforming herself into someone quite different from the older woman she had met a moment ago on the stairs. The white muslin gown she had worn on arrival was discovered under a pile of other clothing on the bed, and soon Her Ladyship was as girlish as artifice could make her, with her orange curls replete with ribbons.

"Before we go downstairs," she said when she had finished, "I want to ask one question. On just what basis do you assume that I have any further acquaintance with your cousin Jeremy than would be indicated by my friendship with his mother?"

It would be futile, Emily realized, simply to say that she had seen Jeremy and her in close conversation that they clearly did not wish to have overheard. The evidence was far too slight, and now that Lady Randolph had agreed to meet Lord Carrigan, she did not wish to alienate her further. But before she could speak, Lady Randolph had taken another tack. Indeed, she slipped into her other personality, as though in preparation for her descent downstairs.

"Such a peculiar household, my dear," she murmured, fluttering a white ivory fan and her long eyelashes in perfect cadence. "Your aunt is a lovely woman, of course. Always laughing. Indeed, sometimes I am quite sorry. . . . But never mind. What I meant to say is that I do not pretend to understand what is going on." She paused and added, as though she had read Emily's mind, "And, if I spoke to Jeremy, it was only to make inquiry. After all, I had just been shouted at by a gentleman whom I had never set eyes on before. And now you make all sorts of innuendos, or at least you did so when we were on the stairs. Can you blame me for being distressed? And now I must meet your inamorato . . ."

And, although Emily made protest, Lady Randolph continued to chatter on about her complaints as they left her bedchamber and descended to the drawing room.

"La, I do not suppose that he is even attractive!" she said as Bert, the footman, came to open the double doors. "Lord Carrigan, you say. I cannot recollect hearing the name before. But what is this, Miss Brooke? You told me that one gentleman was waiting, not two!"

As for Emily, she let out a cry when she saw that Lord Carrigan had been joined by her father.

"My dear!" George Brooke exclaimed, hurrying to take her in his arms. "I took you by surprise. 'Pon my soul I did! Why, child, it was lonely in the country without you, and, besides, I mean to buy a few stocks on the Exchange."

CHAPTER ELEVEN

"What a surprise it was to find you here when we came back from playing whist," Lady Fairfield told her brother as they sat about the fire in the green salon that evening. Phoebe, plump and almost pretty in the firelight, sat on a footstool at her mother's knee, the picture of content, while Emily was curled beside her father on the settee, wearing the pink and white frock that was his favorite, with her black curls tied up high with a pink ribbon in the way he liked best.

"Why, I almost could not believe my eyes," Phoebe declared.

"It was the nicest surprise I could have had, Papa," Emily murmured, entwining his fingers with her own.

Thirty years ago, having decided that not being the elder son, there was nothing he would like so much as to become a country gentleman, Emily's father had invested himself with the modest title of squire and settled on an estate in Kent that he called Haven Hall, for no better reason than that he liked the sound of it. His father had provided him with an adequate inheritance, and while his wife was still alive, he never touched the capital. But, after her death, desiring to make some part of his life, at least, something of a gamble, he had taken to the Exchange. And, although he remained a doting father and as earnest a manager of his estate as ever, there was often a dreamy expression in his eyes that Emily had learned to recognize as a portent that he was due to go to London.

That look was there now, and, glad as she was to see him, she was bound to wonder what he would invest in next. There was no end to the stories he had spun her about the fortune he would make in silver, gold, and even tin. Once it had been the tusks of elephants, and another time, certain derivatives of poppies. Every mad gamble of trade inflamed his imagination, and now, remembering Mr. Drew's dismal counsel, Emily was forced to wonder how she could best convince her father of the need for caution.

But, in the meantime, it was apparently to be an evening for family confidences, most of which, it seemed, were to emanate from Lady Fairfield, with the cheerful assistance of her Phoebe.

"Only fancy my not remembering her," Lady Fairfield said when she had finished describing Lady Randolph's arrival. "I do not think that I am quite old enough to be going dotty, but certainly my memory is not what it was. The strange thing was that Phoebe could not call her to mind either. She is not the sort of woman you would have thought either one of us would forget. However, she seems a very pleasant creature and clearly does not intend to make a nuisance of herself."

"She is off and away somewhere tonight," Phoebe said, cupping her round face in her hands. "She means to see some of her other friends, no doubt."

"It was odd that she did not mention where she was going," Lady Fairfield murmured. "But there! I do not know what is wrong with me. Where she goes is her own affair, and I am delighted to see her entertain herself."

The squire had let his sister ramble on, but now he held up his hand to indicate a full stop. Emily's father was a handsome man, with grizzled hair that he wore pulled back in a queue. His face was blunt-featured and roughened by the weather, and age lines were beginning to cut deep into his forehead and the corners of his mouth. But his eyes were his best feature, and they were as bright blue and youthful as though he were still a lad one quarter of his age. It was the eyes that gave a hint both of his generous nature and of the high hopes that he persisted in holding out for the future when his ship would come in at last. Now he addressed his sister in a serious voice.

"Do you mean to tell me that the lady whom I met this afternoon, the person who was introduced to me as your guest, is a stranger to you?"

"Well, of course I can't say that, because she knows

both me and Phoebe so extremely well," Lady Fairfield protested.

"You only have her word for that," her brother reminded her. It was so precisely what Emily had wished to say and had not, because she thought it would do no good, that her fingers tightened on her father's and he glanced down at her with an indulgent smile.

"I told Emily that she would not find you the most practical of people," he continued, addressing his sister in an affectionate tone that took the sting from the criticism implied. "And now you have demonstrated that you are too trustworthy by far and, I think, not the best possible judge of people."

Emily hoped that he was not about to refer to Mrs. Burbain, the cook, and Danvers, the butler, and Nelly, her aunt's dishonest abigail. They would know at once that he was only speaking to the point she had made once before, and neither Phoebe nor her mother was prepared to pay any regard in that quarter. Besides, Danvers had displayed an admirable loyalty when he had offered to throw Lord Nicholson out of the house, and Mrs. Burbain had cooked a meal in the Squire's honor that had been eminently succulent. Granted that Nelly was not so easily justified, but no doubt she had some virtues that Emily was not aware of as yet. And so it was with some relief that Emily heard her father begin to elaborate on Lady Randolph.

"In the first place," he declared, "from what I saw of the lady this afternoon, I think she is pretending to be something she is not. And, by that, Alicia, I do not simply mean she is pretending to be your friend, although I think that, too. No. Do you know what made me suspicious? It was not the fact she dyes her hair or layers her face with makeup. That might be explained by the fact that she wishes to look younger than she is. Many ladies do the same, I know."

Under the layer of her own vermillion, Lady Fairfield could be seen to flush a higher scarlet than the one she had applied. But she kept her usual smile on her lips and listened to her brother intently.

"No," he continued. "It was the way her accent slipped and wavered. I have always had a good ear, you know. Emily here can tell you that I can hear a lark a mile away. This lady speaks, for the most part, in the accents of Society, the same accents that rise quite naturally to your lips, Sister, and to mine. I make no special point in our favor in saying that. It is, quite simply, the case. But with Her Ladyship, whoever she may really be, she will drop an *h* occasionally, or allow a certain quality to come into her voice that makes me think she was born rather closer to Bow Bells than one would expect of someone of her rank. Have I made myself quite clear? Not to put too fine a point on it, I believe she is an imposter, Alicia, and I think you owe it to your family to find out who she really is and what she really wants."

"Do you think she might be involved in the matter of the kidnapping, Papa?" Emily asked before her aunt could offer any disclaimer, as she seemed about to do.

"You said that the Duke of Nicholson seemed to recognize her," the Squire said. "And she appeared on the very day that his son was discovered missing. She pretends to being someone I do not think she is and makes an outrageous performance of it. All of which may mean nothing or something. Certainly, from what I have seen of the lady, I would not put anything past her."

"She did behave in the most extraordinary manner this afternoon," Emily admitted. "First, she seemed inclined to play the flirt and, then, because she saw that she was bewildering you, Papa, and irritating Lord Carrigan, who only wanted to ask questions, she became quite haughty and talked about her life on the Continent, where, it appears, she only associated with the most exclusive people."

"I think," Lady Fairfield announced cheerfully, "that she simply must be shy. I've found that people will say the most peculiar things when they feel awkward. I know that I have done it myself."

"And I think, my dear Alicia, that you have been too generous by far in your estimation of this lady. In fact, I consider it my duty to find out more about her than what we know."

"Dear George," Lady Fairfield said hesitantly, "do you think you really ought to pry?"

"Just so, Mama!" Phoebe cried. "One of the things you have always taught me is not to ask too many questions for fear I may not like the answers I receive."

"To whom do you intend to go, Papa?" Emily demanded eagerly.

"Why, Carrigan for a start, I think," the Squire said in a deliberative way. "I had no time to talk to him alone this afternoon. But, damme, if he didn't seem a fine fellow, and he kept a close eye on the lady, just as I did. And then, if he has no clues, I propose to go to Lord Nicholson. From what I've heard of that little scene this morning, I take it that he thought he recognized her. Besides, I propose to know what steps he intends to take against my nephew. Blasted cheek to come here and make accusations!"

Lady Fairfield bounded to her feet like a rubber ball, her face still wreathed in smiles. "Dear George!" she exclaimed. "Always so thoughtful of others! But I really must insist that you do not concern yourself. Consider for a moment, if you will. Does it sound credible to you that Jeremy would be involved in a kidnapping? Is it conceivable that a total stranger would be staying in my house?"

"Mama is right, of course," Phoebe observed. "Why the very notion is so absurd that I can scarcely keep myself from falling into a fit of giggles!"

The Squire raised his eyebrows, looking pointedly at Emily, and she did the same. She knew that he was thinking that he could scarcely intervene in his sister's affairs if she protested. And yet, Emily had the uneasy feeling that one might be sitting on the edge of a volcano that is making threatening noises. Something unpleasant was about to happen. She was certain of it. There had been tension in the air during Lady Randolph's brief interview with Lord Carrigan and her father, although nothing of importance had been said. And there was tension now at this family gathering, from which, significantly, Jeremy was absent.

The Squire had just begun to present his arguments to the effect that his sister and his niece should be prepared to take everything more seriously, when Bert, the footman, announced that Sir Adrian Rap had made them a call. Immediately, Phoebe was all aflutter, rushing to examine her face in the oval glass above the mantel and making a great twitch of her dress and muslin fichu, not to mention her white dormeuse cap. As for Lady Fairfield, she took no notice of the lateness of the hour, but declared that they would be delighted to receive such an excellent friend at any time.

The Squire, who had not had the pleasure of meeting Sir Adrian before, was clearly taken aback when that modish gentleman came mincing into the room, his quizzing-glass held to his eye, quite resplendent, as always, in his embroidered waistcoat, satin coat, and pantaloons, and carrying a gold-knobbed walking stick with a tassel on the top.

"My dear Lady Fairfield!" he exclaimed. "How good of you to receive me. I confess that the hour *should* make a social call out of the question. But, as you can see, I am quite breathless, for I came here directly from Lady Meredith, who is holding a small soiree. Everyone was exchanging news, you see. And I have heard something that you must hear immediately!"

"Now, now, sir, you must calm yourself," Lady Fairfield said pleasantly. "My brother will help you to a glass of wine. You have not met him, I think. Dear George, Sir Adrian is bound to become one of your dearest friends."

Somehow, Emily did not think that highly likely, for not only did her father quite despise gossip, but he was far more conservative in matters of dress and fashion in general than Sir Adrian gave evidence of being. However, he would have helped Sir Adrian to a glass of wine, had not Phoebe arrived first at the decanter and poured with the reverence of one making a libation.

Even in a state of excitement, Sir Adrian did not forget his manners. "Dear Miss Fairfield," he murmured as, blushing, she handed him the glass. "So kind of you. And my dear Miss Brooke. Charming! And just up from the country, too."

This last he murmured under his breath, but Emily, who had heard him say it too many times before, noted every word quite clearly. Neither did she miss seeing the special smile that Sir Adrian lavished on her as he minced across the room and took a chair close beside her.

"Now then," he went on. "What was I saying? Oh, yes. I was speaking with Lady Meredith. She is always au courant, you know. A singularly well informed lady. And she had it directly from Lady Colfax that two gentlemen had been waylaid and attacked in St. James's Square tonight, just as they were leaving White's. I came to offer my condolences, and then, of course, the moment that I saw you sitting around the fire, I knew that you could not have heard."

"I am afraid, sir, that I do not understand you," Lady Fairfield said pleasantly, leaning forward in her chair. "Two gentleman, you say? And do we know them?"

"Oh, dear, Mama!" Phoebe cried. "I am so terribly afraid . . ."

"Explain yourself, sir!" the Squire cried, growing very red in the face all of a sudden. "Why should you have come here to offer condolences? Spit it straight out, sir! Spit it straight out!"

"I am making reference to your nephew, sir," Sir Adrian replied. "To your son, Lady Fairfield. To your brother, Miss Phoebe. He and the Honorable David Carrigan were set upon just as they were walking through St. James's Square, as I said before, and I could find no one who knew the full extent of their injuries."

CHAPTER TWELVE

"Attacked in St. James's Square!" Lady Fairfield declared. "Why, you can scarcely expect me to believe that, Sir Adrian. Such a fashionable part of town! I believe that you are having a little joke at our expense."

"We all know about your sense of humor, sir," Phoebe chimed in.

But, although both her aunt and cousin kept cheerful expressions, Emily could see that they were only tentative and that the slightest jolt would shatter their composure. And, from the look in her father's eyes, she knew that he had seen it, too.

"You know what rumors are, my dear," he said to his sister, going to press her hand. "No doubt there is not a word of truth in what Sir Adrian has heard. No, no, sir. Not another word. We must not disturb the ladies until we are quite certain of our facts."

"Lady Colfax's footman was passing through the square at the time it happened," Sir Adrian babbled on. "And he reported to her quite certainly—"

"Not another word!" the Squire declared with emphasis. "We will be certain of our facts first, as I said before. Why, I cannot believe that we would not have been contacted immediately if this had been the case. Keep smiling, Phoebe, there's a good lass, and make your mother do the same. As for me, I will be off to get the story straight. Which means, I think, I must repair to White's."

"Pray allow me to accompany you, sir," Sir Adrian said. "I will not have an easy moment until I know your nephew is all right."

Emily said nothing, but she went to get her pelisse, only

to return downstairs to find her father and Sir Adrian in the hall, discussing the content of a message that had just been delivered.

"We have heard from Lord Carrigan, my dear," the Squire said. "Your aunt and cousin know nothing of it, since the message arrived just as we were coming out of the salon. I think it might be just as well simply to tell them that Jeremy is not injured seriously and is presently with Lord Carrigan and his brother at their house on Curzon Street."

"I know the place!" Sir Adrian said excitedly.

The Squire successfully ignored him. "Since it appears you mean to accompany us, my dear," he said to Emily, "perhaps we should leave at once and allow Danvers here to take in a verbal message. I should not care to let them see the note, you see, since it does mention that your cousin *has* been injured, and they would only worry. Do you understand what you should say, Danvers? Simply that the young master is safe at Lord Carrigan's and that we have gone to see after him."

"I shall have no trouble conveying the gist of that, sir," the butler said in his informal way. "I do not think it will occur to the mistress to ask if there were injuries, since, as you know, sir, she prefers to make only the most pleasant assumptions."

"This time may be different," the Squire warned. "I think the shock of this may have cracked the shell of her cheerfulness."

"I would not like to think it, sir," Danvers said, pulling a very long face indeed. "I do not mind admitting that I have never worked in a household that was run so much to my particular taste, and I would be sorry to see anything change."

Including, Emily supposed, the right to purloin silver at his discretion. But there was no time to consider petty theft just at the moment. Jeremy and what could have happened to him were the only subjects on her mind. The fact that her cousin was presently at Lord Carrigan's and that she was to go there, too, was of very little consequence, she told herself. Her heart would have pounded just as heavily if they had simply been going to White's as her father had first proposed.

Danvers was just off to the drawing room, and Bert,

the footman, was opening the door for them to depart, when Lady Randolph came hurrying into the house, dressed in a most extraordinary way, for the long, black cape she wore had not even the slightest bit of color to distinguish it, and the hood that was attached completely covered her carrot-colored hair. She let out a startled little cry when she first saw them and then assayed a smile. Murmuring something about it being a lovely night, she hurried off upstairs. The silence was complete, except for the rumbling of carriage wheels up the street, which made Emily wonder whether her aunt's mysterious guest had returned from wherever she had been by hackney cab or had been driven to the door by someone with a private carriage.

"Ah, well," the Squire said, almost reluctantly, as he watched the black-caped figure reach the top of the stairs, "there is no time to speculate about her now. Is that your phaeton at the curb, Sir Adrian? Fine! Fine! Nothing could be more convenient. Now, let us be off to Curzon Street."

Emily was grateful to her father for making no protest when she had indicated her determination to accompany him. He had always given her her independence in the country, and she was pleased to see that the fact that she was now in London made no difference to him. Then too, it crossed her mind that perhaps he wanted her as a buffer between him and Sir Adrian, who, she was certain, struck him as a very odd sort of creature indeed. She could not think what her father would made of Jeremy, who was even more the fop and dandy than Sir Adrian. But, then, she told herself that the fact that his nephew had been victimized would be sufficient to make her father blind to any other details, at least at the very first.

Due to the lateness of the hour and the lack of traffic on the streets, their drive to Lord Carrigan's house did not take very long, although Sir Adrian did his best to lengthen the minutes by describing in some detail a variety of crimes wrought by footpads of late. Emily had been relatively unaware that the streets of this great city were as dangerous as Sir Adrian described them, but she was willing to grant that, given the lack of light at night and the narrow alleys that abounded, more often than not with only old men with staves to patrol them, the likelihood was certainly that crime would be a commonplace affair. What a safe life she had led, she thought, with her goings and comings at nighttime protected by footmen carrying torches and by a closed carriage. But gentlemen were not so careful, and that, no doubt, had been her cousin's downfall. And yet, she had the uneasy feeling that it was more complicated than that.

Lord Carrigan's house was built in the Georgian style, entirely of brick, except for a portico that sported four Doric columns of white. They were admitted by a servant in grey and silver livery and led across a grand, black and white marble-floored hall to the library, where the bookcases rose to the level of two ordinary rooms and the fire, which had been lit against the damp of evening, threw out fingers of light that stroked the calf-bound volumes lining the walls. Lord Carrigan was standing beside a large writing desk, and the single candle that was burning there threw his handsome face into a bold relief.

"Miss Brooke!" he exclaimed. "I had not thought to see you here."

"By that, sir, do you mean that I should not have come?"

"No. On the contrary. I believe that your assessment of the circumstances may prove extremely useful. Squire Brooke, sir. I am glad to see you again, although I might have hoped that we would meet in more pleasant circumstances. And Rap. I might have guessed that you would find some way to be here."

When in search of gossip, Sir Adrian was not easily insulted, and, as a consequence, he responded with a bow, making a flourish with his tricorne hat with the feather in it.

"Your servant, sir," he declared unctuously, making his words curl and coil like oil floating on water. "If there is any service I can render you at this unpropitious moment . . ."

Lord Carrigan made an impatient movement with his hand, and Sir Adrian's voice died away accordingly. "The fact of the matter is, sir," he said, addressing himself to the Squire, "that your nephew and my brother were set upon while crossing St. James's Square earlier this evening."

"You see!" Sir Adrian exclaimed. "I knew that Lady Colfax could not possibly be wrong."

"And who was responsible for this outrage, sir?" the Squire demanded. "Were there witnesses? Can the ruffians be identified?"

"How badly were they hurt?" Emily said in a low voice. "Surely, Papa, that is the first thing to determine."

"Of course, my dear," her father said, putting one arm around her. "But, damme, it inflames my temper to think that such a thing could have happened. Are they badly hurt, Lord Carrigan?"

"Your nephew's arm was broken," the young Marquess replied. "The physician finished setting it not ten minutes ago. As for my brother, he was badly bruised in the scuffle. And, as for witnesses, there were none. That, at least, I have determined. As for identification, we will have the two victims with us shortly. As soon as the physician has completely settled with them, they will be sent down. In the meanwhile, Miss Brooke, may I offer you a glass of ratafia? I know this must have been a shock. And, gentlemen, a glass of claret?"

Emily and her father were soon ensconced, glasses in hand, close to the fire, which was welcome on a damp night. Lord Carrigan took his position by the mantelpiece, and Sir Adrian, in his excitement, seemed unable to stop mincing around the room.

"Certainly, Lord Carrigan," he said, "robbery must have been the motive! Tell me, was either of the young gentlemen carrying large sums of money. I know the way of the world, you see, and that must certainly have been the reason they were set upon."

"The opposite would seem to have been true, sir," the Marquess replied dryly. "The only things they carried in their pockets were various duplicates of bills of indebtedness, which they had managed to incur this evening in a matter of a few hours while gaming at White's. Of course, the toughs who attacked them may not have known this."

The Squire cleared his throat. "Nothing more natural, I suppose, than that it should have been assumed that they had won a packet," he declared.

Lord Carrigan smiled with a degree of irony. "That would absolve the scoundrels of knowledge of the identity of their victims, at least," he said. "I cannot remember a time when my brother has left White's a winner, and, although I cannot speak for a certainty for your nephew, sir, I believe the same may be true of him."

"But if robbery was not the motive, what could it have been!" Sir Adrian demanded, coming to a pause long enough to drink deeply from his glass.

It was then that Emily spoke. Her voice was low but clear, and she sat very straight in her wing chair, a slim figure in white, her dark curls tumbling below her bonnet. "Is it coincidence, do you think," she said, "that Lady Randolph should have been returning to my aunt's house, just as we left it, in a clear state of agitation and wearing a black cloak?"

Her eyes met Lord Carrigan's and, for a moment, no one spoke. "I think that lady bears investigation," he said finally. "She was out tonight, you say? And did she inform your aunt of where she intended to go?"

"My aunt said that she respects Lady Randolph's privacy," Emily replied. "The answer, sir, is no."

"My sister has certain peculiar little ways," the Squire began, only to be interrupted as Jeremy and the Honorable David Carrigan came into the room. Two more pitiful sights Emily thought she had never seen, yet, at the same time, there was something absurd about it, perhaps because they were so thoroughly cowed. Gone was all of Jeremy's foppishness, for not only had his shirt and coat been cut away to allow the doctor to get at the swollen arm—which was swathed in bandages from his shoulder to his wrist—but somehow he must have lost his high-heeled red shoes, and he was walking in his stockinged feet. His blue satin pantaloons were covered with mud, and the Brutus cut of his hair, of which he was so proud, had assumed a sadly rumpled appearance.

As for the Honorable David Carrigan, his fair-haired handsomeness had been severely marred by cuts and lacerations, which had left his face bruised and swollen. One eye was almost shut, and over this he held a piece of red beef, which was dripping on his cheek in a most unattractive way. His clothing, too, was disarranged, and, when he opened his mouth to speak, Emily saw that he had lost a tooth.

"Well, gentlemen," Lord Carrigan said. "What have you to say for yourselves?"

"Surely you are rather hard, sir!" Sir Adrian exclaimed. "Why, this is a shocking thing, sir. A shocking thing! To think that a gentleman cannot be safe steps away from his own club!"

"I think you would do better to allow Lord Carrigan to handle matters, my dear Rap," the Squire said in a low voice, "unless, of course, you wish to give him cause to ask you to go."

That suggestion was quite sufficient to make Sir Adrian clamp his mouth quite firmly shut, although he continued to peer at the two victims through his glass for all that he was worth.

"Jeremy," the Squire continued, "tell me, my boy, do you recognize me? It has been a good many years since you have seen me and you were only a lad then. I am your Uncle George, boy, and I am sorry to find you in this unfortunate condition. Surely you can give us some explanation."

But before either Jeremy or the Honorable David could say a word, the door to the library flew open, and Lord Nicholson elbowed his way past a footman to lead the way into the room. And in one hand he was holding a scrap of paper.

"Another message," he declared in his resounding voice. "This one just delivered to my door by a rapscallion of a boy who ran off straightaway. I was informed that I should come to your house, Lord Carrigan, and that I would find here two gentlemen in the condition my son will soon be in, if I do not hand over the five hundred pounds directly!"

CHAPTER THIRTEEN

He was, Emily thought, in a less bombastic mood than
when she had seen him before. Indeed, he even paused
long enough to allow her father to be introduced to him,
although he studiously preferred to ignore Sir Adrian. As
for Emily herself, he extended her a nod. But it was,
quite naturally, no doubt, for the two young gentlemen,
still standing just inside the door like schoolboys waiting
for the headmaster to punish them, that the Duke reserved most of his attention.

"Damme, but you two are a sorry sight!" he muttered.
"Someone is up to no good. No doubt about it."

Lord Carrigan moved out of the shadows. "This should
convince you, sir," he said to the Duke, "that your suspicions were unjust. Clearly these fellows cannot be both
the perpetrators of the crime and the victims of it all at
the same time. And that note, which you hold in your
hand, is ample evidence, I believe, that whoever it was
who kidnapped your son was responsible for the attack
that was made tonight."

Lord Nicholson did a great deal of hemming and haw-
ing, punctuated with the occasional "Damme" and " 'Pon
my soul," all of which he seemed to consider quite a sufficient apology.

"David," Lord Carrigan said, approaching his brother,
who was still applying the beefsteak to his eye in a woe-
begone manner. "Did you recognize the men who set upon
you?"

His brother shook his head and mumbled that it was
too dark to see.

"But if you were in the Square," Lord Carrigan argued, "there must have been a good deal of light from the houses all around you, and most of them have torches set out. It was not after midnight, when, I agreed, it might have been impossible to see unless there was a moon."

Emily took note of the fact that his brother would not look him in the eye and that her cousin, too, was staring at the carpet.

"I told you that we could see nothing and that is the truth," the young man repeated. "We were set upon. That is all there is to it."

"For money?" the Squire said. "Did they pick your pockets, Jeremy?"

But Jeremy was to prove just as uncooperative as his companion. He could not remember, he said. He was so engaged in trying to protect himself, that they may have rifled his pockets a score of times and he would not have taken notice. Furthermore, he added, even if they had, they would have found nothing, not a shilling.

"You left a string of promissory notes behind you, I presume," Lord Carrigan said. Then, adding quickly, "No matter. The important thing is to discover the connection between the attack on you and the kidnapping of Lord Nicholson's son. We can assume, sir," he went on, turning to the Duke, "that these two were chosen to be victims because of their friendship with your son. Furthermore, whoever did this thing knew something of their habits. All of which suggests . . ."

"Go on, sir!" the Duke demanded.

Lord Carrigan shook his dark head. "I must think on it," he said. "An idea has come to me, but I think I must develop it."

It was clear to Emily, at least, that in Lord Carrigan's opinion, the two young men were lying, and she was inclined, on the basis of their behavior, to agree. It was the moment and the time to arrange the scene in such a way that certain revelations, voluntary or otherwise, would take place. And yet it seemed that no one, including herself, knew how to proceed. It would be better to strike out in the first direction that came to mind, she concluded, than to let this opportunity pass. And, therefore, she gave voice to the unexpected.

"Lord Nicholson," she said, not without a certain sinking of the heart, "I hope you do not think this is beside the point, but I wonder if you could explain to us why seeing Lady Randolph at our house this morning seemed to cause you such dismay. I will be frank, sir. My aunt has taken her in on trust that she is who she says she is and that they were, indeed, once friends. But I have reservations, and I would like to know what you can tell me about the lady."

It was clear from the furious frown the Duke turned on her that he was not accustomed to being challenged in such a way by anyone, let alone someone of the opposite sex. "Dammed bit of sauce, gel," he replied, "to think I would answer such a question. And what's it got to do with the business at hand, eh? What's Lady Randolph, if that is what she calls herself, got to do with that?"

By the time he had finished, his voice had risen to such a roar, that Emily had to fight the temptation to put her hands up to her ears. Still, she found the bearlike gentleman did not frighten her as much as she had thought he would. There was a good deal of bluster in him, certainly, but she did not think it went very deep. She remembered how easily her aunt had tamed him that morning, at least until Lady Randolph had come into the room.

"There is no need for you to speak to my daughter in that tone of voice, sir!" the Squire retorted angrily, advancing with his fist clenched and his weatherbeaten face screwed into a frown. "If you persist, I will demand satisfaction."

Lord Carrigan stepped between the two older men and, although both of them were of a good size, he stood taller than either. "We have injured gentlemen enough in this room already, my friends," he suggested with a hint of dryness in his voice. "I think Miss Brooke's question was quite suitable."

As he spoke, his eyes went to his brother, just as Emily's flew to Jeremy. And so it was that they saw the two young men look at one another and a distressed expression flood first one face and then the other. It was time for Emily and Lord Carrigan also to exchange a glance.

"Yes, I am certain that your answer might provide some information that would help to complete the puzzle of a kidnapping and two beatings," Lord Carrigan went on thoughtfully.

"I knew that there was some mystery about Lady Randolph!" Sir Adrian declared, shifting his chair in such a way that he was sitting very close to Emily. "She looked familiar! You will remember my saying that, Miss Brooke."

Emily thought that Sir Adrian would have done better not to remind anyone of his presence in the room. Certainly, if Lord Nicholson were aware of his reputation as a scandalmonger, he would insist that he be put out before he made any revelations. If he made them.

"Oh, very well," she heard Lord Nicholson say. "But there is no connection, I assure you. However, Miss Brooke, your aunt deserves to know that Lady Randolph's real name is Lola Hewlett. At least, that is her professional name when she is acting in comedies on the stage. That is the name I knew her as, when we were . . . when we were friends a good many years ago."

"Friends!" Sir Adrian cried. "My goodness gracious!"

"One word from you outside this room on the subject, and I will wring your neck with my own two hands, Rap!" the Duke declared.

Sir Adrian dropped his quizzing-glass in his agitation. "My dear, dear sir!" he cried in a shrill voice. "May lightning strike me dead if I ever so much as hint at anything you say here."

"You will not have to wait for lightning if you do," the Duke assured him gruffly. "Now, Miss Brooke! Are you satisfied? Or is there more you want to know? My personal life is apparently to be your open book."

Emily was too keenly interested in what he had said to bother with the sarcasm. "An actress!" she exclaimed. "And you knew her. You were upset, it seemed, about seeing her again."

"And with damned good reason, gel!" the Duke of Nicholson shouted. "The jade has had her eyes on my boy! Never mind the fact that he was years the younger. Told her that myself, I did, when I found him with her at . . . hum, hum, I won't go into that. At all events, I called her a cradle snatcher and other words passed. Not a pleasant memory, that. Sight of the chit brought it all back."

Once again, Emily saw Jeremy and the Honorable David glance at one another, and she hoped that Lord Carrigan had seen it, too. Clearly, quite by chance, she had happened on something of importance.

"Did it not seem strange to you, sir," she continued, "that an actress whom you had reason to think of in relation to your son should have turned up under another name in the house of the mother of one of the young men you had decided was somehow involved in your son's kidnapping?"

Lord Nicholson lowered himself into a chair. "You must give me a moment to think that out, Miss Brooke," he said in a far more conciliatory manner. "Yes. Yes. I see. It is too great a coincidence. That is what you are getting at, I believe."

"I knew that I had seen her somewhere before!" Sir Adrian crowed delightedly. "It all comes back to me now. But her hair was black then, surely, and not that peculiar shade of orange."

"Doubtless, she considers herself wearing a disguise," the Duke replied. "Lola was never long on brains, if you take my meaning. But she was a greedy little thing, and although she may be getting a bit long in the tooth, she still looks a sight when she is kicking up her heels on the stage."

"I remember her when she played Clarinda in *The Suspicious Husband!*" Sir Adrian cried. "Why, it was worth the price of admission just to watch her prance about the stage!"

"Gentlemen!" the Squire announced in a loud voice. "I beg you to keep in mind that there is a lady in the room!"

But Emily had been too engaged in thought to know or care about the details of Lola Hewlett's manner on and off the stage. She bit her lip and looked at the Honorable David and her cousin and tried to pull the strands together. It was a pity that nothing had been said thus far that was sufficiently alarming to make one of them speak out involuntarily. Perhaps, she thought, she should have another try.

"Yes, Lord Nicholson," she said, "it is too great a coincidence. Let us grant the fact that one day, out of the blue, an actress named Lola Hewlett decides to change her identity, for no particular reason. Granted that she decides to pose as a member of the aristocracy and spin a tale about having been abroad. Granted that, by dyeing her hair orange and wearing gowns that would better suit an eighteen-year-old girl, she thinks that no one will recognize her. You *did* say, did you not, sir, that she was not long on brains? Well, taking all of that for granted and adding to it the fact that she apparently once tried to seduce your missing son, Lord Nicholson—"

"Seduce!" the Duke roared. "I did not say that! 'Deed I did not, Miss! What a word for a gel to use! Damme, if I'm not shocked."

Emily saw Lord Carrigan smile. And, as a consequence, it was easier, somehow, for her to persist.

"I only mean to make the point that Lady Randolph, as she calls herself, may be the missing link that would make some sense of all of this," she said. "And, if that is true, I think that someone should talk to her seriously. Someone should shock her into telling us what she is up to."

"A truly inspirational idea!" Sir Adrian declared, taking Emily's hand, apparently for the purpose of kissing it, did she not snatch her fingers away. All of which did nothing to discourage him, for he went on at some length to state his admiration of her.

"Enough!" Lord Nicholson roared. "Not that I'm not of a mind to agree with you, Rap, but I will have nothing to do with the jade."

Emily became aware that Jeremy and the Honorable David Carrigan appeared to be edging toward the door.

"I'll speak to her in private," Emily said in a voice that was strong enough to carry across the room. "And I will do it tonight. Jeremy, you know the lady slightly. Do you think that will be a good idea?"

Having, in this fashion, focused attention on the two battle-scarred young gentlemen and, as a consequence, having halted their attempted flight, Emily had the satisfaction of hearing her cousin mutter that it was no concern of his.

"I am afraid that may not be the case," Emily heard Lord Carrigan mutter, but in so low a voice that she did not think the others heard. And she knew that he was thinking, just as she was, that there was a great deal more to this affair than met the eye.

CHAPTER FOURTEEN

It was nearly midnight when they returned to the house on Cavendish Square. Jeremy, suddenly loquacious, gave Emily any number of reasons why she should not disturb Lady Randolph that night. This advice was suspicious in itself, since Emily had never seen prior signs that her cousin spent any time at all in consideration of other people's feelings. But the Squire, not knowing the young gentleman as she did, was inclined to be impressed and gave it to Emily as his opinion that she should not press the matter without some consideration.

"You know you are inclined to be headstrong, my dear," he said in a conciliatory voice. "It cannot be endured, of course, that the woman remain in my sister's house wearing a false identity. I shall protest strongly against that myself. But perhaps it would be just as well to wait until the morning, child."

But, as it happened, there was no need for Emily to come to a decision in the matter, for one of the first things Lady Fairfield informed them of when they reached the house, was that her dear friend, Lady Randolph, had left.

"She said that she had something urgent to attend to," Phoebe declared. "And do you know, I do not think that she would even have come to tell us she was leaving, if I had not happened to meet her on the stairs. She had got Bert and Danvers to carry her portmanteau for her by promising them a guinea each, or some such. And then, after they had hailed her a hackney cab and all the rest, she rode away without so much as giving them a shilling. They were that put out, I assure you, and made a great

99

rumpus about the way they had been treated until Mama tipped them both."

All this information was delivered before Jeremy had come into the hallway, since he had lingered behind, groaning slightly as he descended from the carriage, as if his bruises were troubling him, as no doubt they were. But the moment that he stepped into the light and his mother and his sister, both in dressing gowns with their hair hidden under nightcaps of magnificent proportions, saw his condition, there began a great outpouring of sympathy and offers of ministrations of every variety. Finally, despite his protests, Phoebe hurried off to fetch a hot stone for his bed and his mother to fetch a certain powder that was guaranteed to make him rest, while Danvers, who was summoned by Lady Fairfield with an unusual peremptoriness, was sent to take a decanter of brandy to her son's room and Bert was told to help Jeremy up the stairs.

"So our Lady Randolph is gone," the Squire muttered. "Somehow, my dear, that does not take me by surprise."

"Jeremy and Lord Carrigan's brother are beaten up by footpads tonight. She returns to this house shortly after it must have happened, wearing a black cape. And then she disappears," Emily reflected aloud.

The Squire cleared his throat. "I hope that you are not implying that you think the lady was directly responsible," he said. "Lord Nicholson said that she was a jade, and I have no doubt that that is true. He also implied that she was empty-minded, which does very little to set her apart from ladies in general, in my opinion, although I know that you will not agree. But nothing that I have heard about her has led me to believe that she would either have the inclination or the energy to knock two young and energetic gentlemen about St. James's Square and leave them in the condition we have observed tonight."

Emily could not help but laugh at that and tell her father not to be absurd. She knew, of course, that he had said it expressly to soften her disappointment that she could not have the interview she planned to have. He was as aware as she that, once set on a certain path, it was a great frustration to her to be prevented from continuing.

Kissing her father, she went upstairs herself, all the

time thinking of her part in all of this. What did it matter to her if Lord Nicholson's son had been kidnapped? Of course, she was sorry enough for it, if it were true, as it increasingly seemed to be. But she did not know the Duke, or at least she had not until this morning. What a very long time ago this morning seemed to be!

Passing Jeremy's room, Emily could hear him grumble as his mother and sister fussed over him. And, the door to Lady Fairfield's bedchamber being partly open, Emily saw Nelly, her aunt's pert abigail, going through the contents of a jewelry box in a practiced and discriminating manner.

Emily's first impulse was to catch the girl in the act and make an accusation, but then she remembered that she had promised to let her aunt handle her own affairs. Doubtless, if she said a word about what Nelly was doing, the abigail would raise a great fuss, and, before it was over, Lady Fairfield would have paid her a tip or something of the sort for having been troubled in the process of stealing.

So it was that she cleared her throat and shuffled her feet about before she entered, only to find that Nelly, in supreme self-confidence, had not even troubled to make an attempt to disguise what she was doing.

"How much do you think this topaz is worth, Miss?" she inquired. "I know my way about well enough with diamonds and sapphires and the usual sort of thing. But a topaz is exotic like. Unusual, if you take my meaning."

Emily replied that she took her meaning very well and asked how it happened that Nelly was still up and about, to which she received the response that Nelly prided herself on always being about when Her Ladyship might need her.

"And, after all the fuss and pother there has been to-night, one way or the other," she declared, "the mistress will want to be waited on just so before she goes to sleep. Not that she'll ask for favors, mind you, such as having her pillows plumped and the water in her pitcher just the right temperature and such. She's too good a sort for that. 'Go to bed, Nelly, do,' she said to me just now, when she and Miss Phoebe came helping the young gentleman up the stairs. I tried to help them with him, but he told me to shove off in an ugly way. I don't mind telling you,

Miss, that there's nothing I wouldn't do for the mistress, and Miss Phoebe too, but the son will get himself into bad trouble, if he hasn't done so already. Mark my words if that's not true."

Quite suddenly, Emily saw Nelly through fresh eyes. Like Danvers, who had offered to throw the Duke of Nicholson bodily out of the house that morning because he thought he might distress his mistress, Nelly was dedicated, too. And yet both Nelly and Danvers stole from her. The incongruity of it struck Emily with so much force, that for a moment she forgot what she had come in to say. Then, as it happened, Nelly, who was in a loquacious mood, reminded her of it.

"There's a lot going on that I don't understand," she declared. "Take the lady who appeared out of the blue and said that she was staying here. At least she *said* she was a lady, although I have my doubts. She had the accent nearly right, you see, but it *would* slip and slide now and then. And she didn't have a lady's ways. Why, she hadn't been in her bedchamber ten minutes before it looked as though a storm had struck the room. And what lady would dye her hair a color like that, I ask you, and pretend to being under twenty, when the truth of the matter is there to see for anyone who looks her in the face? Not that she wasn't a hand with the vermillion and such. It was a treat to watch her put it on. Like watching Gainsborough or one of them fancy painters, I shouldn't wonder."

It had been Emily's idea to question Nelly about their brief and mysterious guest, but the abigail soon made it clear that she did not need a single question to start her torrent of opinion and information.

"Dropping in here without a word of advance," Nelly said scornfully. "And all that talk about being just up from Dover. I recognized the jarvey who drove her here, see. He operates his hackney in the city and nowhere beyond. She didn't come from Dover any more than I did, and I tried to tell the mistress so, but you know how she is, Miss. Why, she would let herself be robbed blind and not say a word."

At this, she had the good grace to blush, but directly she recovered her equanimity. "And there was another thing that struck me, Miss," she said. "I've a notion something was up between her and the young master. I like to keep my eyes open, you see, and my ears too, when necessary."

"What did you hear?" Emily asked quickly. "Tell me, Nelly, for I think that it may be important."

The abigail was thrown into a thoughtful mood. "I wouldn't like to cause any trouble, Miss," she said finally. "Not for the mistress nor Miss Phoebe, at any rate."

It was all that Emily could do to keep from asking the girl why, if that were true, she helped herself to their jewelry and trifles. Perhaps, she thought, Nelly suffered from kleptomania. Perhaps she could not help herself. But that was a subject that must be tackled another day.

"You must believe me that it will be to their advantage to know as much as possible about the lady who was visiting here," she said. "I can explain no further, but I hope you will believe me."

"Well, Miss," the abigail replied. "I won't pretend that I could make head or tail of what I overheard, but it had something to do with that Lord Nicholson who made such a fuss here this morning. Danvers told me all about it, so I recognized the name. A duke or some such whose son is missing. Kidnapped, Danvers said. At any rate, the lady and the young master were having words about it. Quarreling like, you understand. She said that it was not her fault that something had gone wrong, and there was mention of someone called Tanker. An odd name that, I thought. She said he was bound to make trouble if he didn't get his money directly."

"And is that all?" Emily demanded. "Try to remember everything you heard."

"Well, Miss, they began to talk low after that," Nelly explained. "I pressed my ear to the door ever so hard, but still—"

She broke off, flushing, realizing, no doubt, that she had drawn the difference between overhearing and outright eavesdropping rather more clearly than she had wished.

"It doesn't matter, Nelly," Emily assured her. "As it happens, it's just as well that you were curious. The name Tanker may be of some help to me."

Nelly, who had always seemed so pert to Emily before, was demonstrating a serious side of her nature that could not have been guessed at. Perhaps it was the lateness of the hour, or the fact that unsettling events had taken place that lent a special earnestness to her expression as she rose from the dressing table and followed Emily to the door.

"There isn't anyone who works here who don't want to help Lady Fairfield and Miss Phoebe any way we can," she said in a low voice, all of her usual flippancy cast aside. "We keep our ears open, all of us. It's not just me. That's how we happen to know about her trouble financially. The tradesmen don't know, as yet. But that was what the gentleman with the spectacles wanted to talk to you about, wasn't it, Miss Brooke? Bert happened to be passing by and—"

At that point, Emily did not think she could resist making a demand to know why, if the staff were so sympathetic, they persisted in robbing their mistress at every turn. Either they were the greatest group of hypocrites ever gathered in a single house, or this was all part of the most cruel joke she had ever heard of.

But just as she opened her mouth to speak, her aunt and Phoebe bustled in the door. "He's sleeping now, poor darling," Lady Fairfield crooned. "The poor, dear boy, but it could have been worse. I have just been telling Phoebe that we should be very grateful that it is not worse. Dear Jeremy will be quite his old self again in a day or two."

Nelly echoed Emily's sentiments of relief that this was the case and indicated that she was willing to fetch her mistress something from the kitchen if she needed to be refreshed. Tea being mentioned, she hurried off with a promise to return directly and help both of her ladies to bed.

"Dear Nelly," Lady Fairfield said with a weary smile. "I think the world of her, I do, indeed. She came to me without a reference, you know, like all the others. Her last place was with Lady Newcome, who refused to give a reason for dismissing her. So unkind, I think. It raises so many questions, and people are always bound to think the worst. Nelly had been three months without a situation before she came here."

It was exactly like her aunt, Emily thought, to have weathered an evening during which a mysterious guest had disappeared without a word of explanation and her son had been beaten by ruffians and yet to talk about something as apparently beside the point as Nelly's problems.

"Did Jeremy mention anything to you before he went to sleep?" Emily asked. "I mean to say, did he give you any idea why he and his friend were set upon? He would say nothing when we were at Lord Carrigan's."

"No doubt my dear boy is suffering from shock," Lady Fairfield reflected. "Why, I do not believe he really understands what has happened to him. That is the way of it, they say, when something terrible happens or you are badly hurt. Nature has a way of making you not feel it, which is so very sensible, I think. But then nature usually *is* sensible. It is only when we begin to turn and twist it out of shape that it plays awkward tricks on us."

"And Lady Randolph," Emily began, "what do you make of her departure?"

"Really most peculiar," Lady Fairfield said, sitting down at her dressing table and removing her turban. For the first time, Emily noticed that her aunt was not as young as she always liked to see her, and she realized that without her cheerfulness she would be quite old and ordinary. The notion was unexpectedly painful. She had meant, of course, to tell her that the so-called Lady Randolph was, in fact, an actress who sometimes appeared in comedies. Indeed, she had meant to go further and confide in her aunt her conviction that not only did Lola Hewlett, as Lady Randolph should more properly be known, know Jeremy, but it appeared that there was some plot between them and that the plot might very well be involved in some way with the disappearance of Lord Nicholson's son.

But now she knew what she should have guessed before. Her aunt saw the world as something very different from what it really was and Phoebe was the same. They bounced their way through life, plump and cheerful, never guessing that they were being taken advantage of in a hundred ways. But could it be that underneath their smiles there were two potential tragic masks? Because if that were so, Emily, for one, did not intend to be responsible for stripping away their smiles.

And so she said good night, leaving them to the care of Nelly, knowing that they were in good hands. There was a light under her father's door, and Emily found him already in his dressing gown, studying a small pile of papers by the light of his bedside candle.

"A peculiar thing that," he said, kissing her good night. "I mean Jeremy being beaten up the way he was and that business about Lady Randolph, or whoever she really is. I must talk to Alicia about it tomorrow."

"Don't tell her any more than she asks to hear, Papa," Emily begged him. "I think she truly doesn't want to know."

The Squire nodded his grizzled head. "She's been that way since she was a child," he mused. "And now her daughter's like her. Good of you to understand, my dear. I think you're right, you know. What good would it be for her to be exposed to the whole sordid story? For that will be what comes out in the end, damme if I'm not certain of it. Yes, sir, a sordid story, and her own son at the very heart of it. Mind you, that's what my intuition tells me. I don't know about the facts. And now, my dear, scoot off to bed. It's late. It's late. Tomorrow I want to tell you about a marvelous opportunity I have to invest in a diamond mine somewhere in Russia. I can't remember just where it is, at the moment, but I have it in these papers somewhere."

The last thing Emily thought that night, before she fell asleep, was that she sometimes felt very lonely, as though there was something different about her. The truth was that she was fond enough of Jeremy, and yet she could not understand why he preferred to live the way he did. And much as she adored her father, she thought he played the fool every time he thought of the Exchange. Granted that she had a better understanding of her aunt and Phoebe than she had before, yet she did not know why they were as they were. In fact, she felt as though she did not understand anyone in the whole, wide world, including Lord Carrigan. But she would not think of him! And, doing so, she fell asleep.

CHAPTER FIFTEEN

"Your father was off ever so early," Lady Fairfield declared, pouring herself a cup of morning tea, while, beside her, Phoebe applied herself with her usual attention to a pile of scones and a very large pot of honey. "He means to have a word with his solicitor, you see—you know Mr. Drew, don't you, my dear?—And then he will be off and away to the Exchange."

"Diamond stocks," Phoebe declared. "He told us all about it, and Mama and I mean to buy a few. Uncle George has said that he will advance the money for us to do so."

Emily heaved a deep but silent sigh. She had depended on being able to talk to her father this morning to prevent him from taking any precipitate financial action, but now, having overslept, she found she was too late.

"Dear Mr. Drew," Lady Fairfield remarked, allowing herself a third spoon of sugar for her tea, "the poor gentleman will worry so. 'It is not good for your health,' I tell him. But he cannot help himself, I think. Why, to listen to him, you would think that we were nearly penniless. Is that not so, Phoebe? Have I exaggerated?"

Phoebe patted her rosebud mouth with a linen napkin. "Exactly so, Mama. And when Uncle George makes us little loans from time to time to see us through the next quarter, you would think we had committed some sort of crime in accepting. Still, I like Mr. Drew all the same."

"He means well," her mother chorused.

"He has our best interests in mind."

"But he certainly is far from cheerful. I often wonder if we are not far more of a trouble to him than we are worth," Lady Fairfield declared. "I believe I could manage our finances myself if I were to turn my hand to it."

A little shiver ran up Emily's backbone as she thought of the disaster such a step would be, and she made such mild protests as she could bring to mind on a moment's warning.

"Well, well, my dear, no doubt you are quite right, and it would be too great a responsibility," her aunt agreed. "Besides, there is the problem of mathematics. I could never do even the simplest of sums, you see, and Phoebe has taken after me in that."

Having said which, she gave her daughter a proud smile as though she had just handed her an accolade of the highest order.

To change the subject and because she truly wanted to know, Emily asked about Jeremy, only to discover that he was feeling a great deal improved and that he spoke of coming downstairs and, even more incredible, of leaving the house that very morning for some business or other.

"I told him that he should not consider it," Lady Fairfield said with a smile, "but you know what young men are. So resilient! A message was brought around from Lord Carrigan's young brother quite early. I do not know what was in it, but Jeremy made such a face and tore it into shreds. When I left him, he was dressing with Bert's assistance. I have tried and tried to convince the dear boy to have a valet of his own, but he says that no decent servant would come into this house and rub shoulders with those who are already here, although what he can really mean by that, I do not know."

How easily her aunt appeared to be able to forget what had happened, Emily thought. Of course, Lady Fairfield was not prepared to consider that the scuffle Jeremy had been involved in had been anything more than an accident. The footpads who had attacked them might have attacked anyone leaving the club at that particular time on that particular night. But Emily did not believe that convenient theory. She guessed that Jeremy and the Honorable David Carrigan had been chosen as victims for a very particular reason. The message that had come from Lord

Carrigan's brother this morning seemed to indicate that something was still going on, something that gave Jeremy no pleasure. He planned to go out today as soon as he was able. Unless she did something to stop him, no doubt he would be in so much trouble that even his mother could not ignore it.

Consequently, Emily made her excuses and left the breakfast table to go upstairs to Jeremy's suite of rooms. Bert, the footman, was just coming out into the corridor when she arrived at the door, and he stood for a moment looking at her and letting a long whistle stream through his teeth.

"The young master's in a temper," he told her finally. "You wouldn't credit the things he said to me. If I hadn't come out when I did, I would have whopped him one in the jaw, if you'll pardon me for saying so, Miss Brooke. I wouldn't go in there if I was a lady like you and all. The language isn't suitable, for one thing."

Bert had served a term in Newgate Prison for a crime that had slipped Lady Fairfield's mind. That was all that Emily knew of him, except for the fact that he looked the part, with a cast in one eye and two black teeth at the front. But he always seemed to be going about his duty in a serious sort of fashion, and she thought it would be a true irony if the only member of the staff apparently not engaged in larceny of some sort was the one among them who certified as a hardened criminal.

"Thank you for warning me," she said and smiled in such a way to show she meant it. "But if he is preparing to go out, I think that I must speak to him directly. Tell me first, however, did he happen to let drop anything to you about what happened yesterday?"

"He said that someone he knew would get what they was owed and that he didn't mean five hundred pounds, either," the footman replied. "He's in a pugnacious mood this morning, Miss, although you wouldn't think he would be, beat up as he must have been last night. It's a strange thing, that. Your average footpad likes an alley better then a well-lighted square. Of course, the young master does dress so fancy that you might think his pockets would be heavy with a bit of tin."

"Yes, yes," Emily said. "That must be it, of course. But did he say anything else about what happened? It's important that I know."

Bert considered her and pulled one ear. "Nelly did say as how you were taking an interest, Miss," he said. "I call that right good of you. Her Ladyship is a saint, you see, and saints don't see what's going on, if you take my meaning. That Lady Randolph, for example! What a joke that was from the beginning! Why, she was no more a lady than me, Miss. Not that one. But the young master must have been taken in."

Emily dropped the knob of the door. "Why do you say that, Bert?" she demanded in a whisper.

"Because he wrote a note to her this morning early," the footman replied, "and had me call a boy to take it around."

"Take it around where?" Emily asked insistently. "You can't have forgotten the address!"

"Happens I have, Miss," Bert replied after much rolling of eyes and other facial contortions, which were, she took it, meant to help. "Not a street I was familiar with."

"Well then," Emily said, trying to control her excitement, "what about the boy?"

"He was just one of those lads that stop about on curbing, Miss, waiting for an errand to run or a horse's reins to hold," the footman told her. "They're never in the same place twice, you know. Here today and off working Piccadilly tomorrow. This square's too quiet to keep them long, Miss."

"Very well, then," Emily said, and her blue eyes took on a determined look. As Bert told them later in the kitchen, she was just a slip of a thing, but he shouldn't want to come between her and what she thought was right. It may be that Jeremy made much the same sort of evaluation as she came into his sitting room and stood quite quietly by the door—a slender figure in a demure blue- and white-striped morning dress, with a blue gauze fichu, and blue ribbons on the white mobcap that only partly covered her dark curls. At all events, he did not exactly welcome her with open arms.

"No time for chats, Cousin," he said in a defiant voice. "I know you take yourself very seriously, but be assured that I do not, and that I found your attitude last night at Lord Nicholson's to be absurd if not ridiculous."

"It would be difficult for it to be one and not the other," Emily observed tartly. "And by my attitude, you mean my stated intention of interviewing Lady Randolph, as we knew her, I presume."

"Your implication that I might know the woman did not go quite unnoticed by me," Jeremy replied. "I never did like the sort of gel who pokes her nose into everything with total lack of discrimination, the type who often go begging for a husband."

"If that is the sort of barb you think will affect me, Cousin," Emily declared, "you have sadly underrated my intelligence."

The gauntlet had been thrown down between them, but it did not appear that Jeremy was prepared to remain for the battle. Dressed a la mode in tight-fitting, calf-colored breeches reaching to just below the knees to meet his white silk stockings, not to mention the single-breasted coat of superfine with the tails ending just above the knees, and the waistcoat, vertically striped in the current fashion, he had awkwardly been putting the last touches to his cravat with his left hand, and now, while Emily was still speaking, he gathered up a silver-knobbed cane and a civilian version of the Swiss, military-type hat called the Kevenhuller.

"You must excuse me, Cousin," he declared, put slightly out of countenance, no doubt, by the fact that Emily had planted herself directly in front of the door.

"I will do so gladly," Emily replied, "if you can assure me that you do not intend to continue to put yourself in a position that might bring your mother shame or embarrassment."

"I cannot think what is in your mind," Jeremy replied.

"Lady Randolph is in my mind, for one thing," Emily replied. "Or should I call her Lola Hewlett? Which name does she usually go by with you?"

"I did not know the lady until she appeared in this house and introduced herself, as it happens," Jeremy replied, and Emily noticed that a nerve beneath his right eye had begun to twitch. "I was as much surprised as anyone to hear that she was an actress, and I am totally confused as to why she chose to come here for her brief stay. If you like, I will inform my mother . . . but, no doubt, you have already done so."

"She appears to have forgotten Lady Randolph," Emily replied. "The danger you were in put her completely out of mind, I think. There is no need to remind her of it or make her nag her mind to solve the mystery of why the woman came. When we have the answer to it, perhaps it will be different. Time to tell. But not now."

"You have a penchant for protecting her," Jeremy said with an unpleasant smile. "She is a good deal stronger than she appears, Cousin, I assure you. She sees precisely what she wishes to see and no more. There is no need at all for you to appoint yourself as her protector."

It was precisely at that point that Emily decided to jar him out of his complacency. "Do you know a man named Tanker?" she demanded coolly. "I believe he is a friend whom you and Lady Randolph have in common."

Jeremy's face was still so black and red with bruises that it was difficult to be certain whether he turned pale, but clearly he was taken aback.

"Tanker?" he said. "Why should I possibly know anyone called Tanker?"

"That is what I wondered," Emily retorted, "which explains why I asked the question. Has he anything to do with the kidnapping?"

Jeremy began to pace up and down the room, nursing his damaged arm. "Listen to me, Cousin," he said in a conciliatory voice. "The only thing I know about the kidnapping is that young Nicholson was apparently with me before he disappeared. I've told you that I was in my cups and that I do not remember anything that happened after he and I left Ranelagh Gardens. Now, you may believe me or not, just as you choose, but that is the truth of the matter."

"I only wish I could believe you," Emily said sadly, "but I do not."

"Think of it this way," Jeremy went on. "Nicholson and his father never did get on. He may have disappeared because of some quarrel or other."

"In that case, how do you explain the ransom note?" she asked him.

"Damme, I am not even certain that there is or ever was a ransom note!" Jeremy exploded. "Has anyone beside the Duke actually seen it? Have *you* seen it? Read the words, I mean?"

Emily recalled the slip of paper that the Duke had taken from his waistcoat pocket and read to them. It had not occurred to her to doubt its contents, and she could think of no reason why she should doubt it now.

"Why would he have made up anything so preposterous?" she inquired. "And then, there was the second message, which came after you and your friend had been set upon, warning him that if there were no payment, his son would receive precisely the same treatment."

"As far as I know, no one ever saw that note either," Jeremy replied.

"Are you saying that the Duke had something to do with the attack on you and David Carrigan?" Emily demanded. "Are you saying that he takes the occasion of his son's disappearance, first to level charges of conspiracy at you, and then to have you beaten up in St. James's Square?"

"I did not say anything of the sort!" her cousin shouted. "I can make no more sense of it than you can! But I think you should stay out of it. Indeed, I strongly suggest you do!"

"Is that a threat?" Emily asked him.

"Perhaps it is!" Jeremy replied, so out of temper that, as Emily thought later, he might have said anything at all. "And now, I warn you, if you do not remove yourself from that door . . ."

Emily realized that she had gone as far as she could at the moment, and perhaps a good bit further than she should have gone. Clearly, Jeremy was in such a frame of mind as to make him capable of pushing her out of his way which, with only one able arm, he could do quite easily.

And so she let him pass, and, as he hurried down the stairs, muttering to himself, she went to the long window at the end of the hall to wait and to watch him go into the street. She had not noticed Bert duck back against the wall when the door to Jeremy's rooms opened and subsequently follow the young master down the stairs. But she saw the footman from the window and wondered what he was about, for, as Jeremy strode out of the square, Bert was behind him. Only when they both had turned the corner and disappeared, did it occur to her that she might have gained a useful ally, who was as interested as she was in discovering just where Jeremy's business was taking him.

CHAPTER SIXTEEN

No sooner had Emily seen the last of Bert than a hackney cab drew up outside and Mr. Drew descended from it in a clear state of agitation. By the time she had hurried down the stairs, he was asking Danvers for her. In order to avoid interruption, she asked the solicitor to join her in the library, which, because of Lady Fairfield's and Phoebe's indifference to books, remained the most unused room in the house.

"I suppose you have seen my father," Emily said before he could begin. "I know about the diamond mines, but he did not give me the time or the opportunity to attempt to dissuade him. Besides, you can scarcely imagine the confusion of events here."

"Yes, yes. The matter of Lord Nicholson's son," the solicitor said, polishing his spectacles. "I have heard no more about that in the past twenty-four hours, so I expect it is fair to say no charges have been brought against anyone. But, in this matter of your father . . ."

Emily could see that his interest, just at present, was completely engaged by her father and his intended visit to the Exchange, and therefore she determined not to distract him by mentioning the exodus of Lady Randolph or the attack on Jeremy and Lord Carrigan's younger brother. Doubtless, he was not interested in details of that nature anyway, but only in the possibility of legal suits and the proper handling of his client's money, as in the case of her father.

"I have done my best to put him off," Mr. Drew continued, "and I wanted you to know, Miss Brooke, in the hope that you can offer me assistance. The amount he wanted to invest is staggering. If he is to lose it, it will mean the end for him financially, and there will be no more assistance for your aunt. I handle her affairs as well, you see. But then, you know that! I cannot seem to think straight this morning. To think that your father would want to do such a thing! He says he has it from someone quite reliable that he will stand to realize a fortune! He says there will never be a better opportunity—"

"Calm yourself, Mr. Drew," Emily implored. "You said that you had put him off."

The solicitor's hands were shaking as he placed his spectacles carefully on his long, sloping nose. "I have delayed him," he replied, "which is all that I can do, except to offer him reason, which, by the way, he rejects out of hand."

"What have you done exactly?" Emily demanded, marveling to herself that even the serious, practical-minded Mr. Drew could have been reduced to such a bundle of nerves. London would break anyone in time, she decided. No doubt that was why Lord Carrigan had advised her to be cynical on the one hand and then, soon after, had implied that it would somehow spoil her, had hinted that she was tainted with it already! But then, what choice was there, except to do as her aunt and niece and father had done and keep one's hopes ridiculously high?

"Why, I have told him that there will be some legal problems in touching his capital any further," the solicitor went on. "But he will find out I am hedging sooner or later. His banker will explain it to him if someone else does not. The best we can hope for is a delay of a few hours or, perhaps, of today. I came to see you, just as I did once before, to implore you to intercede before it is too late. These diamond mines—if they exist at all, which is not so very certain—will fail him, just as everything else he has ever purchased at the Exchange has done. I am fond of your father, Miss Brooke, even though he lacks business acumen, and, as for your aunt, she needs someone to protect her."

Emily smoothed the full skirt of her gown thoughtfully. "Papa has never talked to me in any great detail about his investments," she replied. "Oh, he will mention that we are about to become wealthy whenever he buys new stocks, and then, later, he will be quite bewildered when it all falls through. But he has a dream, you see, that he will amass a fortune, and he has had it for so many years that it may be he will never give it up until there is no more to lose."

"That day is rapidly approaching," Mr. Drew assured her. "He always gets his tips from a certain old gentleman at his club, who seems to possess an unerring sense for the truly bad investment. The Marquess of Harmond, I believe he's called. Apparently, he has more money to lose than your father has. But that is by the by . . ."

"No!" Emily exclaimed. "Just on the contrary! I met the gentleman once, you see. At my first ball at Lady Courtiney's. He was so very kind and he did say he knew Papa, but I never guessed that he might be responsible for our financial difficulties."

"I would go and see him," Mr. Drew declared. "Implore him not to give your father tips. But if the Squire ever heard of your visit . . . I mean to say, he is good-natured to a fault, but there are limits, and I would not like to lose his friendship with my interference."

"Let me write to Lord Harmond!" Emily said, rising to go to the escritoire in the corner and take up a quill. "Do you mind waiting, Mr. Drew? I would like your opinion as to whether or not I put it well. Then, if you are satisfied, I will send it off at once. The letter will, I think, find Lord Harmond at his club. I will simply explain the circumstances and ask to see him. Perhaps I can persuade him that Papa cannot afford his well-meant advice."

She had no sooner finished the communication and given it to the solicitor to peruse, however, than her father's voice was heard in the hall, sending Mr. Drew into a state of consternation, which Emily relieved by withdrawing with him to the adjoining sitting room and from there to the back hall, where steps lead down to the servant's entry.

"There are certain days when everything goes wrong," Mr. Drew said, so far forgetting himself as to take off his periwig and wipe the bald dome of his head with his handkerchief, "and this is one of them. But you have phrased your message to the Marquess well, I think, and I will see to its delivery for you. After that . . . well, we will have done all that we can do. Good-bye for now, Miss Brooke. No, no. I will see my own way out."

And, muttering to himself, he left the house, while Emily, pausing only to take a very deep breath, indeed, and hope a silent hope that Lord Harmond was a reasonable man, went to find her father, who was now sitting with her aunt and cousin Phoebe in the green salon.

" 'Damme, Mr. Drew,' I said to him," the Squire was saying as Emily came into the room. " 'It's my money, after all, and I should be able to get at it when I want!' But do you think that he would listen to me, even when I told him that there was a fortune waiting to be made? Not he! Some legal matter or other concerning the estate, which has to be taken care of. And there's crafty old Harmond buying up every stray stock he can lay his hands on. But there's no good fretting about it, I suppose. Besides, I shall go to my bank tomorrow and let them have it out with Mr. Drew, I'll be a gudgeon if I don't. Emily, my dear! I was talking so hard I did not see you come into the room. Come and give your old father a kiss."

"Now. Isn't it nice that we are all together!" Lady Fairfield exclaimed. "I expect Jeremy will be down in a minute, and we will have a cozy time of it. Phoebe and I have just been going over this month's order of stores with Mrs. Burbain. What a treasure that woman is! I declare, I never check her figures, although she says she would like me to."

"The soul of honesty," Phoebe added, with such a contented smile that, thinking of the Thursday afternoon deliveries, Emily felt her heart drop. What a pleasant place the world would be if people like her aunt and Phoebe could keep their illusions, and optimists of her father's ilk could have their ships come in, indeed, instead of always going out.

Instead, she knew that she must tell them that Jeremy had gone out on business. Later, she must do whatever she could to convince her father not to gamble any further with his capital, no matter how excellent the diamond mines might sound. Everywhere she turned, grim reality made its appearance, and Emily found herself wishing, for a moment, that she had her aunt's and cousin's ability to turn her back to it.

But before she could mention Jeremy, Sir Adrian was

ushered into the room, evoking a little cry of joy from
Phoebe and a warm welcome from Lady Fairfield. The
Squire was a little more reserved, and Emily, when confronted with the gentleman's familiar leer, greeted him as
coolly as good manners would allow. With everything she
seemed to have on her mind, she could have done without this visit, and she was thinking of excuses to leave the
room, when she was alerted by something Sir Adrian was
saying.

"It is the common gossip," he was saying, "that Lord
Nicholson has decided not to pay the ransom, at least,
not right away. I have it, straight from someone who
ought to know, that he has concluded that this is as good
a way as any to keep the lad on tenterhooks for a while.
They never got on, you know, and His Lordship did not
care for the young gentleman's acquaintances. With a few
exceptions, of course," he added, coughing a bit and looking quickly around the company.

"But surely that is dangerous in the extreme!" Lady
Fairfield cried. "I am certain you must be mistaken. News
never makes its way to more than two or three people
straight. I'm sure that, on the contrary, if he has decided
not to pay, it is only because he knows that it is all a
prank."

Emily hoped that Sir Adrian would not be drawn into
an argument reminding her aunt that the bruises Jeremy
sported were real enough to indicate that there was jeop-
ardy abroad. But he seemed quite content to ladle out information until he had reached the bottom of the bowl.
And then, she suspected that Sir Adrian would want whatever news they could give him and was happy that she
had not yet had the opportunity to tell them that Jeremy
had gone abroad.

"Actually, I suspect that Lord Nicholson was so impressed with you, Miss Brooke," Sir Adrian went on with
a gush of words, "that he intends to wait until you have
spoken to Lady Randolph before he takes a step. I suppose one should call her Lady Randolph as long as she
is in the house, although if a spade is to be called a
spade—"

"But Lady Randolph is no longer here, Sir Adrian!"
Phoebe exclaimed, just as Emily had been afraid she
would. Her cousin was wearing a pink taffeta polonaise

gown, which made her look quite charming, although perhaps a bit plumper than usual. Beside her, Lady Fairfield, wearing the brown- and yellow-striped costume that she favored, looked more than ever like a bumblebee.

"She came and went so quickly that there was scarcely time to renew our old acquaintance," Lady Fairfield said reflectively. "However, no doubt she will drop in on us again. She seems to be a lady of an impulsive nature."

"But is it possible, Madam," Sir Adrian began, "that you do not know—"

"My aunt knows everything she cares to know about the affair, sir," Emily interrupted, before he could go too far.

Sir Adrian examined her with his quizzing-glass, and for the first time she noticed how sharp and black his eyes were. "I see," he said, in a voice that told her that he understood. "But perhaps you will permit me to inquire, my dear Miss Brooke, if you had time to have a conversation with the lady before she left? You are the center of a good many people's interest, you know. Lord Carrigan's. Lord Nicholson's." He clicked his tongue against the top of his mouth and added, sotto voce, as though talking to himself, that she was just up from the country.

"My daughter did not have the opportunity to have her interview," the Squire said. "It is good that Sir Adrian reminded us, my dear, that there are others who will be interested in hearing that the lady left this house so precipitately."

Sir Adrian rose from his chair and bowed to the Squire or Emily or both. "Allow me to convey the news," he said. "It will give me an excuse to see both gentlemen today. Nothing could be more convenient, I assure you."

"Sir Adrian is always so very thoughtful," Lady Fairfield told her daughter.

"A most congenial gentleman," Phoebe replied.

"Your daughter, Squire, is quite a delightful creature," Sir Adrian said archly. "One would never think she was just up from the country. Oh, no, indeed!"

"Sir Adrian presents his compliments so convincingly," Lady Fairfield declared.

"Oh, yes, Mama!" Phoebe replied. "I find it most affecting. Indeed I do."

"In point of fact, sir," Sir Adrian went on, mincing forward as Emily pressed against her father and took his hand. "I would appreciate a word with you in private about a certain matter that is very close to my heart."

And with that, he ogled Emily so openly that she flushed, and her father cleared his throat in an irritated way.

"Dear Phoebe!" Lady Fairfield whispered. "Only fancy! Sir Adrian wants to speak to George. Of course he *would* go to him as the man of the family. He wants to ask permission to speak for your hand. You may depend upon it."

"Oh, Mama!" Phoebe replied, her plump hands clasped together. "How exciting it will be to be offered for by such a perfect gentleman."

"Allow me, Squire," Sir Adrian was saying, "to suggest that we repair to the library for our private conversation."

"I suppose I cannot refuse the gentleman, Emily," her father muttered.

"It makes no difference either way," she told him. "I am quite indifferent, I assure you. But there *is* Phoebe . . ."

"Dear Sir Adrian," Lady Fairfield said, rising and bouncing toward the door in her brown and yellow gown, "there is no need for you and my brother to go to another room. We ladies know when we are not wanted. Phoebe, Emily, come. Let us have a little chat in my sitting room upstairs until it happens that someone is wanted here in this room again."

And, with that, she swept them out of the green salon with a happy smile and meaningful little glances, which were meant for Sir Adrian but which he did not appear to see.

"Now, be quite confidential, gentlemen," Lady Fairfield announced as she closed the doors with glee. "Oh, Phoebe. I am so happy for you. Indeed I am, and so, I know, is Emily."

CHAPTER SEVENTEEN

It was a situation that Emily did not know how to deal with. Clearly, her aunt believed that Sir Adrian was, at this very moment, offering for Phoebe. As for Phoebe herself, she was radiant with happiness. What would happen when the call did not come for her to go back downstairs? What would happen when it became apparent that Emily was the object of Sir Adrian's devotion?

But, as it happened, that moment never came, thanks to the arrival of a message, which Danvers himself brought up to Lady Fairfield.

"The boy who brought it said that no answer was required, Madam," he said in his dulcifying way. "But he did add that he had been told to say that it should be brought to your attention immediately. Those were not the words he used, of course, him being only one of them street urchins, but I have made a translation which is, I think, close to the mark."

Following this announcement, Danvers did not retire, but stood looking on with undisguised interest as Lady Fairfield broke the seal and spread the letter out before her. And, as she read, the smiling mask fell from her face, and Emily saw the look she had dreaded to see, a look of absolute misery.

"What is it, Mama?" Phoebe cried, clearly frightened. "Why are you looking that way? Oh, dear Mama. Is the news so dreadful then? Shall I call Jeremy to support you?"

"Your brother is not in this house," Lady Fairfield said in a voice that caught and broke at every syllable. "At least he cannot be, if this message was brought to the door . . ."

"I assure you that it was, Madam," Danvers declared.

"He left the house over an hour ago," Emily said in a small voice. "I meant to tell you. He said he had some business to transact."

"This—this note is in his handwriting," Lady Fairfield said, just managing the words.

"Indeed it is, Madam," the butler said, taking the liberty of reading it over her shoulder. "I would recognize the young master's writing anywhere. He has an odd way of crossing his t's."

"But what does he say, Mama?" Phoebe cried, falling to the floor in a none too graceful manner and clutching her mother's knees. "I must know what he says."

Lady Fairfield might have grown ten years older in an instant. Even her plumpness seemed to retreat, and she no longer even slightly resembled a contented bumblebee. "Your brother has been kidnapped, my dear," she said. "There can be no mistake, because he writes it himself, and he would not be so cruel as to play this sort of trick. It must have been true, all of it, although I tried my best not to believe it. Lord Nicholson's son *was* kidnapped. And now Jeremy and Lord Carrigan's younger brother are in the same predicament. He says that they are safe for the time being, but that if Lord Nicholson cannot be convinced to submit to the ransom demand, all of them will be the worse for it."

It was too long a speech for her to have made in her condition, and she slumped back in her chair in a half-fainting position. Emily hurried to fetch the vinaigrette, and Phoebe burst into tears. As for the butler, Danvers, he made comforting sounds and patted Lady Fairfield's shoulder, quite as though he were a member of the family. And when Nelly came into the room wearing her mistress's finest set of pearls around her neck, she seemed to grasp the urgency of the situation immediately and took to applying a handkerchief to Phoebe's eyes and treating both her and her mother in a most solicitous manner.

"Will you permit me to take this letter down to Papa?" Emily asked her aunt, having given the vinaigrette over to Nelly, who was applying it to Lady Fairfield's nose with admirable skill.

But it was too late for that. Having apparently heard something of the commotion, the Squire came puffing into the room with Sir Adrian mincing behind, his eyes beady with curiosity. Clearly, it did not matter a whit to him that he was penetrating an intimate family gathering, and, although Emily was perfectly prepared to ask him to leave, Phoebe made this an impossibility by falling toward him in such a way that he was forced to throw out his arms to catch her or to have her fall, face first, on the floor in front of him.

"Oh, dear Sir Adrian!" Phoebe cried. "Jeremy has been taken! Kidnapped! Held against his will! What are we to do? You must advise us, Mama and me! You know London so well. Oh, we depend on you to prevent a tragedy!"

This little speech was clearly not the sort that Sir Adrian was accustomed to hearing, and his face lit up with delight. Not only had he been offered the most delectable news imaginable, but he had been complimented in such an extravagant way as to clearly be touched at the core of his being.

"Now, now Alicia," the Squire was saying meanwhile to his sister. "Do not give way completely. This may not be as bad as it appears."

"I think that it is worse," Lady Fairfield said tragically, pushing aside the vinaigrette. "I have always been a fool, George, and so have you in your own way. I overlooked so much in order to pretend that this world is a lovely place in which to be. I would not look the horrors in the face, but now there is no way to keep from doing so. I do not think that I will ever smile again."

And, having made this announcement, she slumped in her chair as though she were a very old woman indeed, and tears came streaming down her cheeks, taking the vermillion with them so that they looked like drops of blood.

"Oh, poor Mama!" Phoebe cried. "She will never recover from this blow, Sir Adrian! Only look at her. Whatever can I do?"

Far from attempting to untangle himself from Phoebe's embrace, Sir Adrian seemed quite touched that he should have been called on to support her in such a literal fashion.

"Tell her that it will all come right," Sir Adrian replied.

"I am not without influence in this city. I am well known to certain magistrates and other people of importance. I will make it my business to see that your brother is returned to this house directly."

"I knew I could depend on you!" Phoebe cried, her plump face glowing with trust and admiration.

Sir Adrian preened himself and took both her hands in his. "There are a great many things I can do," he said in an important manner. "After they are done, I will take pleasure in telling you about them. And now, my dear, I must be about my business. Or should I more properly say *our* business? Your brother will be safe, depend on me."

"And I will be off to see Lord Nicholson," the Squire announced. "He is a wealthy man, and all that is needed, apparently, for Jeremy's release, as well as that of his son, is the payment of five hundred pounds. I will offer to put whatever money I can raise at his command. And make a compassionate appeal, as well. Anything to convince him that this is no safe game to play."

After the two gentlemen were gone, it became apparent that Lady Fairfield had collapsed completely. Danvers assisted Nelly in carrying her to bed, while Phoebe hovered about, assuring anyone who would listen that Sir Adrian would be certain to set things right. Indeed, so distressed was Emily by her aunt's collapse that she found herself echoing the same assurances, although she had reservations about Sir Adrian and was afraid that her father might simply send Lord Nicholson into a rage.

Phoebe had just gone in to her mother for a moment, leaving Emily alone in the little sitting room, when Bert appeared in the doorway and demanded to know, in his colloquial way, what the matter was.

"I am so glad to see you!" Emily exclaimed, whirling him out into the hall and closing the door to guarantee a private conversation. "Am I right? Did you decide to follow Jeremy?"

"Now there's no need to be flying up into the boughs, Miss," the footman declared. "There's no harm in my taking a little stroll. As I like to tell Her Ladyship, it's good for staff morale to let them take the stray half-hour off on occasion."

He grinned at Emily, exposing the full glories of his

blackened teeth. "Now that's the story I'd stick with, if I was the ordinary sort. But I overheard a bit of what went on between you and the young master, and I think the more you know about his whereabouts and what he's up to, the better all around. Especially as it seems he's gone and got himself in trouble."

"More trouble than you may know," Emily said grimly. "It seems he's being held for ransom. We got the note not ten minutes ago, and Lady Fairfield is in a frightful state."

"Kidnapped is he!" Bert explained, staring at her in his disconcerting, walleyed way. "Well, he's been quick about it. I'll give him that. Given the fact that he went straight from here to meet up with Lady Randolph, or whatever she may be calling herself now."

"Tell me what happened," Emily demanded.

"I take it this isn't the sort of thing you want your aunt or your cousin to overhear, Miss."

"Yes, yes, Bert! Of course you're right." In her excitement, the color had risen agreeably high in Emily's face, and her eyes glistened. "Where do you suggest we talk."

"I've always fancied the drawing room," he replied. "I mean to say, I'm acting as a friend just at the moment, ain't I? The sort of friend you'd offer a chair to and perhaps a little nip of wine?"

Had matters not been so urgent, Emily would have laughed. There was something about this footman that indicated a strong imagination. No doubt that was what had brought him here with no other reference, except the single comment by a previous employer that she would not trust him across the room. Still, if he wished to be entertained in the drawing room, under the conditions she meant to oblige him.

It did not take Bert long to make himself as comfortable as though he were master of the house. Indeed, had it not been for his livery, Emily might almost have imagined him several degrees above himself in station. And as for his walleye, it would have made him look a criminal even if he had not been one.

"Well, Miss," he began, helping himself from the decanter on the table in the corner, "it all began when I happened to overhear—"

"You listened at the door," Emily corrected him, remembering to smile. "It's just that if you are accurate in little things, it will help to guarantee that you will not elaborate on more important matters."

"There's something in that, Miss," the footman agreed. "It's part of my philosophy, you see, to keep informed about the family I'm serving. You can't imagine, Miss, how useful that sort of information can be. It only stands to reason, don't it, that the more you know about the people you serve, the better you can serve them?"

"No need to justify yourself, Bert," Emily replied. "You eavesdropped and something you overheard made you decide to follow my cousin."

"Well, Miss," the footman replied, "it wasn't so much *what* I heard—although it was that interesting, all this about Lady Randolph being someone called Lola Hewlett and a kidnapping and all—as it was the young master's general tone."

"What do you think of my cousin, Bert?" Emily asked him. Suddenly, it seemed to her that it was important to ask that question and to have an answer. "Be quite honest with me," she added. "What you say will be worth nothing if you are not honest."

Bert cocked his head and surveyed the ceiling. "The young master's a good lad at heart, I think," he said at last. "But he's that selfish. I won't try to deny it. Been spoiled by his mother. That's the way of it, I reckon."

"Do you think that he is capable of criminal activity?" Emily demanded.

"Well, Miss," Bert said, "I should like to think we all are. It would be a terrible thing indeed if only a few of us were blessed in that particular direction."

Emily saw that she could get no further if she followed that tack, as her sense of morality was quite different from Bert's. "Very well," she said. "You followed him because of his tone, you said."

"Something told me he was up to no good," the footman replied. "And I thought I'd keep an eye on him for the mistress's sake. And it appears that I was right, if he has been kidnapped like you say. Although I never would have guessed it could happen so quick like. One minute talking to Lady Randolph and the next minute whisked away."

"Talking to Lady Randolph!" Emily exclaimed. "Tell me what you mean!"

Bert took a moment to empty his wine glass and pour himself a bit more fine claret. There was a certain relish about the way he savored the wine, which told Emily that he was no stranger to it. Indeed, there was something in the way he picked up the decanter, which told her he was not doing that for the first time.

"They'd planned the meeting," Bert told her. "That was clear straightaway. The young master, he sauntered down to St. James's Park, and there was a carriage waiting on the Mall side. I got myself positioned so that I could see inside, because it was clear he meant to join them after he'd talked for a few minutes. Seemed angry, the young master did. Shaking his fists and carrying on. Pity I couldn't hear the words."

Emily had begun to pace up and down the room in her excitement. "Did you recognize the others?" she asked. "I take it there were others beside Lady Randolph in the carriage."

"Two beside," Bert assured her. "A young gentleman with his face all black and blue like the master's and a mean-looking fellow. Not of the same class, that's my guess. Made me curious, he did. Ugly look about him. You see a lot of chaps like him at Newgate."

"Go on!" Emily exclaimed. "Go on! What happened next?"

"Well, I moved a bit closer, which meant crouching behind a hedge. The last thing I saw of the young master, he was getting inside the carriage. After that, I had to stay down on my hands and knees and hope to hear something or other."

"And did you?" Emily demanded. "Oh, Bert, do say you did!"

"Well, the lady referred to someone called Mr. Tanker," the footman told her. "To be exact, she said that no one made a gammon out of Mr. Tanker."

"Tanker!" Emily cried, remembering what Nelly had said about hearing that word pass between Lady Randolph and Jeremy during their conference in the library.

"And then the lady gave the driver the address they was going to. Dill Street, it was. I know the place. It's off the Strand. Why, Miss, I don't know what you're up to!"

To something of her own dismay, Emily discovered that she had actually blown him a kiss. And then she decided to blow him another, as she started toward the door.

"You shall never lack for references in the future," she assured the startled footman. "I shall see to that myself!"

CHAPTER EIGHTEEN

Dill Street was little more than an alley running off the Strand in the opposite direction from the river, and was lined on either side by flat-faced brick houses, which were so precisely like one another as to challenge discrimination. Five of these soot-grimed residences stood facing five others, and the end of the alley was a cul-de-sac. Simply to enter Dill Street was to put oneself in such clear view as to make an unexpected arrival impossible, in Emily's consideration.

"We are no further along than we were before, I fear," she said to her companion, "since we do not know the number of the house."

"Why, Miss, I'm a great hand for tracking," Bert replied. "Like an American Indian, don't you know? Just you wait here out of sight at the turning and I'll investigate."

"But if one of them looks out the window, you will be seen," Emily protested. "I confess that now we are here, I wonder if we have not set ourselves on too dangerous an enterprise."

"There's nothing to this part of it, Miss," the footman protested. "All I've to do is to pull down my tricorne over my eyes and pull my collar high and keep my head down and it's all done up brown."

"But what will you be looking for as a sign?" Emily asked him, pulling the blue cape she had flung on more tightly about her.

"I'll tell you that, Miss, when I find it," Bert declared, and, with that enigmatic remark, was off, looking to Emily so suspicious both in appearance and demeanor, that, had she been a resident of any one of the houses he was investigating, she would have called for the constable at once.

No doubt, she told herself, it had been absurd of her to come here with only Bert as her companion. But when he had told her that he knew where Jeremy had gone and she realized that, according to his description, Lord Carrigan's brother was with him, she had wanted to rush off straightaway. The fact was that when she had heard that her cousin had apparently gone voluntarily with Lady Randolph—the name she still gave Lola Hewlett—and the man named Tanker, she had thought nothing of danger, but only that it all must be a prank. And she had considered further that a great scandal might be made and hurt her aunt, if it could not be quietly resolved. It had gone hard enough by Lady Fairfield to have been told that her darling son was kidnapped. If she should discover that it was all some sort of foolish game and that she had been put through agonies for someone's amusement, her disillusionment would be complete.

As a consequence, it had been Emily's notion that a resolution might be accomplished quietly and with the utmost speed. She would simply confront Jeremy and tell him it was time to put an end to this ridiculous affair. But now that she was actually here, there was something— perhaps the grim, sullen quality of Dill Street, which stood so ominously quiet in contrast to the hustle-bustle of the busy Strand—that gave her pause.

Still, having come this far, she did not like to turn back without interviewing her cousin and seeing what this was all about. And certainly, Bert was keen to continue.

"Move while the iron's hot, Miss," had been his response when she had indicated what her intentions were. "That's the way. There's many a trail has gone cold while people dawdle about and try to make up their minds what to do."

The archway under which Emily was standing was dark and drafty, which must have been the reason that she suddenly felt like breaking into a fit of shivers. But she tensed herself against doing so and pulled the hood of her cape forward until it quite hid the pale oval of her face. Meanwhile, Bert, who appeared to be examining the cobblestones of the street, made his return and joined her.

"For my money, it's number three," he said, pointing in the direction of a house that was different from the others only in that its windows were blank and bare, which made it look uninhabited.

"What reason have you for thinking so?" Emily demanded. "I should think it was the least likely spot, since no one appears to live there."

"Well, Miss," the footman said, "when I was doing my investigation in the park, I happened to notice that there was a deal of mud along the edges of the Mall, on account of the shower we had this morning. Now there's mud just there, and it is from the wheels of a heavy carriage like the one I saw the young master getting into. Fresh mud, Miss. The sort that could have been left there within the hour."

"Very well," Emily replied, aware of a tightening of her breath. "Now, I shall simply go up to the door and ask to see my cousin."

"I mean to go with you, Miss," Bert said, fastening her with his good eye. "No, I insist. Just as you said on our way here, it may be a prank. But then again, maybe it's not. There's always that consideration. And I don't intend for any harm to come to you. That's flat!"

Seeing that it would do no good to protest, Emily did not even try, although she knew they must make a strange sight making a call together.

But when they reached the door of number three, they found it ajar, and, for a moment, they simply looked at one another.

"You see, it really is an empty house," Emily murmured.

But Bert had sharper ears. "Just listen, Miss," he said, putting his head to the opening. "There's someone there. I can hear their voices. Perhaps if we were just to step inside, we might hear something that would put us on the right track. I mean to say, the more we know, the handier we can pull this off."

Under other circumstances, Emily might have been amused to think that she and the footman had apparently become equal partners in this enterprise. As it was, she decided to depend on the man's superior knowledge of criminal activities, including housebreaking. Circumstances had conspired to bring her here at this particular moment, and she would be a fool not to take advantage of the opportunity. Besides, if Jeremy had gone willingly with Lady Randolph and the others, there could be nothing dangerous about all this.

Her signal to Bert was a smile. Slowly he pushed the door more widely open, and they slipped into a narrow hall. To their left, stairs ran to the upper story, and to their right, there was a closed door. But it was from a back room that the voices were coming and so, following Bert's lead, with her cape pulled tight around her, Emily inched down the hall.

Although she could not see into any of the rooms, she had the notion that the house was quite unfurnished. Certainly, the hall had a neglected air about it, and there was not a picture or a mirror on the walls. Somehow, this made Emily feel less conscience-stricken about having let herself in uninvited. This was no one's home, but simply a place to rendezvous, and she and Bert were simply joining the meeting in an unofficial sort of way.

Bert had come to a full halt now, next to another closed door, and Emily saw him hold his finger to his lip. Lady Randolph was speaking, or rather, the actress who had briefly played that role as a guest in the house on Cavendish Square. There was nothing stately about her accent now, and her tone was a far cry from the girlish one that she had employed in her interview with Lord Carrigan the day before.

"We've wasted enough time as it is, Tanker," Emily heard her say. "What's needed is for everyone concerned to know that we are serious. We've had no answer yet from either Lord Carrigan or Lady Fairfield, and I want to know what you intend to do about it."

The sound of a man's rough laughter followed, and Emily knew she was listening to the man whose name Nelly had heard Lady Randolph mention to Jeremy. At the same time, her heart began to sink. At first, she had taken it for granted that her cousin and Lord Carrigan's brother would be in the same room with the two she was overhearing, and there had been comfort in the thought of Jeremy's safety. But now she was somehow certain that the actress and the man named Tanker were alone together. In which case, where were the three young gentlemen who had disappeared?

"You're the impatient sort, ain't you, Lola?" a hoarse voice demanded. "Them notes haven't been sent out two hours yet. Damme, if it's not less than that."

Emily could hear the sound of movement, footsteps on bare floorboards. "If you don't pull this off, Tanker," Lady Randolph said in a voice which sounded ragged with rage, "I'm through with you, you know. I told you at the start it was too big a gamble. But you always have your way, don't you? You're a bully, Tanker. You always have been and you always will be."

"Go ahead and fall into the stewpots if you want to, Lola," Tanker replied. "It's the actress in you makes you fly off the handle."

"Actress!" Lady Randolph cried. "That's it, precisely. I *am* an actress, and if I had been wise, I would have remained one. This little idea of yours may go off sideways, Tanker, and there'll be the devil to pay if it does."

The man's voice suddenly became cajoling, and he muttered a rougher sort of endearment, which made Bert look back at Emily over his shoulder and show his black teeth in an embarrassed grin.

"It happens that you're getting too long in the teeth to sing and gad about on stage," Tanker continued. "Don't look at me that way! It's God's honest truth, and I thought you had agreed to face it. We need a bit of tip to put away to keep us in our old age. And, if we pull this off, I'll make an honest woman of you just the way I said I would."

There was the sound of something that might have been a little scuffle, and Emily wondered if Lady Randolph were fighting off an embrace. Certainly, when she next spoke, she did not sound as though she had been completely mollified.

"I still say," she announced, "that it was a needle-witted thing of you to do to put us in a situation in which we had to rely on anyone as uncertain as those three young gentlemen have turned out to be. Carrigan doesn't seem to care for anything and Fairfield is a fool."

Inconsequentially, Emily thought how furious Jeremy would be if he could hear himself described that way. Certainly, it was proof he was not in the room. She could only hope that Lady Randolph and Tanker would go on talking until they revealed the whereabouts of the missing gentlemen. Already she had learned that there apparently had been some sort of collaboration involving her cousin and Lord Carrigan's brother.

"Well, Lola, my little lobcock, there's no need to worry about either of them now," Tanker declared. "You must admit it was a clever idea on my part to think of how convenient it would be to spirit them away just as we did Nicholson. At least we can be certain they will keep quiet, which was more than we could count on before. And we can make a bit extra on them, to boot."

"I never thought they would be so easy to lure away," Lady Randolph replied, and now there was a note of self-satisfaction in her voice. "But then, I haven't been an actress all these years for nothing, have I, my dear? Did you notice the way they bought my story, even though I was obliged to cut the line?"

"All done neat as houses, old love!" Tanker agreed jovially, and a smacking sound was heard.

Bert chose this particular moment to sneeze. Emily had seen it coming. She saw him gulp in his breath and arch his shoulders and pinch his nose between two fingers. But the offending organ would not be silenced so easily, and a resounding "Achoo!" split the silence of the hall.

Directly, Emily headed for the outer door, with the footman close behind her. But they both came to a sudden halt when the man called Tanker announced that he had a pistol and that, if they cared to turn their heads, they would find it aimed directly at them.

CHAPTER NINETEEN

At close quarters, the pistol seemed to Emily to be a very ancient one. Certainly, it was rusty about the barrel. All this she noted when she and Bert were backed against the wall of the dusty hallway and Tanker was standing by the stairs. The front door of the house had been closed and barred now, and their captors eyed them watchfully.

"I might have known you'd be too curious for your own good, Miss Brooke," Lady Randolph—for this was the only way Emily could think of her—said sharply. "Tell me, do you often bring the footman with you on these escapades?"

"He may be posing as a footman," Tanker growled, "but I know the Newgate sort when I see one, and he's a likely candidate. I'll tell you the truth straight out, Lola, I don't like the look of him."

Lady Randolph approached to within a foot of Emily and leaned forward until their faces were very close together. "How did you come to find us?" she demanded. "And don't be coy, my dear. I won't say that Tanker is a good shot, because he isn't, but no one could miss in a hallway as narrow as this one is, I think."

"I followed the young master when he went to meet you in the Mall," Bert declared, before Emily could say a word. "That's the simple truth of it, and now you will oblige me if you will let Miss Brooke go. I'm the man you want, for I'm the man who is responsible."

"Let her go!" Lady Randolph exclaimed. "You must be mad as well as foolish. I am not going to ask you if anyone else knows your whereabouts, because you would only lie. Clearly, if you had mentioned your intentions,

Miss Brooke, someone would have either come in your stead or dissuaded you from such an enterprise."

The lady was not quite as slow-witted as Lord Nicholson had described her, Emily decided, with a little sinking of her heart.

"It may be that we can turn this to our advantage, my dear," Lady Randolph said, turning to Tanker, who was still holding the pistol straight out in front of him with both hands. "I'll grant you this is an ugly fellow. I thought so when I was visiting Lady Fairfield, and I think so now. She does have a strange assortment of servants, but that is by the by. If you will take the fellow upstairs and guard him, my dear, I may profit from a little talk with our little beauty here."

"Why don't we just put him with the others?" the gentleman named Tanker demanded. "You know that firearms make me nervous even at the best of times."

"He's not to be trusted with those young greenheads," Lady Randolph replied. "Before we'd have a chance to turn around, he would have stirred them up into some mutiny or other. Take him up and guard him, Tanker, while I have a little chat with Miss Brooke and decide what to do."

Lady Randolph waited until a clearly reluctant Tanker escorted Bert up the stairs, and then she indicated to Emily that they were to return to the room where she and her friend had been overheard, a room clearly meant to be a sitting room, but completely bare of furniture or other decoration. Rough, grey cloth had been drawn over the two windows, and so, despite the fact that the day was clear, they stood in shadows. Lady Randolph made a great point of locking the door and slipping the key into the bosom of her gown. She was dressed as girlishly as ever, this time in white muslin sprigged with green, partly covered with a paisley shawl. But her orange hair was covered by a matronly green silk turban, which made her look more her proper age.

"Now, my dear," she said in a silky voice, one of the many she seemed able to adopt at will, "how much did you manage to overhear just now?"

"Enough to know that you are responsible for three kidnappings," Emily replied defiantly, "which came as no real surprise to me."

Lady Randolph put one hand on her hip and the other to her chin, all of which constituted a condescending pose. When she had played at being Lady Fairfield's visitor, she had been girlish. Now she seemed to be attempting the role of a femme fatale.

"You pride yourself on your cleverness, no doubt," she said. "When did you begin to suspect, my dear? It would amuse me so much to know."

Emily sensed that it was to her advantage to encourage the making of this conversation. It might just be that she could persuade the actress to have done with this particular charade. Some sort of bargain might be struck.

"You will remember the night that my cousin and his friend were beaten up." Emily replied. "When my father and I returned from Lord Carrigan's and heard that you had left so unexpectedly—"

"Ah, that was careless of me, I suppose," Lady Randolph interposed. "Indeed, I will be glad when this escapade is over. It has been nothing but a worry to me from start to finish. The night that young Nicholson proposed it to Tanker and me—"

"It was not your idea, Madam?"

"Do not interrupt me, pray!" Lady Randolph exclaimed. "I am an actress, my dear, and I cannot bear an interruption. What was I saying? Oh, yes. I was talking about the worry of it. The night you speak of is an example. The footpads we hired to attack the two young gentlemen were only supposed to give them a scare. But they are nothing but ruffians. A bad lot, let me assure you! Never do business with them if you can prevent it. Anyway, they went too far and gave them a real beating. Tanker and I were there watching in the shadows, but, of course, we could not interfere."

"Then, you were just returning from St. James's Square, when my father and I were leaving to go Lord Carrigan's and passed you on the stairs wearing your black cape!"

"Yes, yes! I *was* in a temper, I assure you. No one does their job properly today, no matter how much you pay them. I *did* think that Tanker and I could depend on our friends, but even that has not been possible."

Emily remembered Nelly's comment to the effect that Lady Randolph's accent was not as impeccable as it should be and thought the abigail must have a very good

ear indeed, because, if Emily had not known the truth,
the actress could have persuaded her here and now that
she was a member of the ton. She was certainly a strange
creature, encouraging Tanker to use his pistol at one moment and complaining about services not properly rendered the next.

"Yes," she was saying now, looking thoughtfully into
the middle distance of the shadowy room, as though she
had quite forgotten that Emily was, to all effects and pur-
poses, her prisoner, "that was the real blow, of course.
Your cousin, Miss Brooke, let Tanker and me down badly,
just as the Honorable David Carrigan did. It was their
idea, theirs and young Nicholson's. A handsome chap,
Nicholson, just like his father was years ago. And just as
dependable, I might add, which is to say that that's a
quality they're both regrettably lacking in."

"You know the Duke?" Emily asked, even though she
knew the answer. Anything to keep Lady Randolph talking.

"Know him, my dear!" the actress exclaimed, clearly
put in a good humor by the question. "Why we were the
dearest of friends for quite some time when we were both
younger. La, what a card he was! Of course, toward the
end, his temper had begun to change, and now they tell
me that he will quarrel with anyone at the slightest opportunity. Indeed, his own son has very few good words to
say for him. Why, if he had not been so put out about
something that happened between them, all this never
would have happened."

Emily knew that if she were to be put in a position to
suggest that the three gentlemen already captured, not to
mention herself and Bert, be released as promptly as was
possible, she must know not only what had happened, but
why. Short as this lady might be on brains, Emily had a
feeling that she would respond well to a short and simple
solution to her problems. And if it could be demonstrated
that the idea of the kidnapping had not been hers and
Tanker's alone, there might just be a chance that a solution was conceivable.

"Are you saying that the Duke's son planned the kidnapping himself?" she asked.

"Of course, you won't believe me, but that's the way of

it, precisely," Lady Randolph said petulantly. "Took us in properly, he did, Tanker and me. It was at Ranelagh Gardens, you see, and we were all together—Tanker, the three young gentlemen, and me. We should have known they were too far in their cups to be trusted."

"You mean, Madam, they all contributed to the idea?" Emily asked her. "My cousin, as well as the others?"

"Your cousin's the worst of them, in my opinion," Lady Randolph replied. "That was why I paid your aunt a visit, as a threat. To get him to cooperate. And to keep an eye on him. Of course, after he and the other gentlemen were so badly beaten up, Tanker and I thought it would be the wisest thing for me to leave. But I don't expect you to understand any of this, and, I declare, I don't know why I'm telling you, except that this is all such a muddle, that I wish we were well out of it."

"Perhaps I can help you," Emily said in a low voice, pushing back the hood of her cape. "Perhaps—"

"Help me!" Lady Randolph replied. "You'll ruin me more likely! That's why I've got to think what to do with you. Here now! I've an idea. We'll cut off those handsome curls of yours, Miss Brooke, and send them to—let me see —why, to Lord Carrigan, of course. That should infuriate him sufficiently to see that Tanker and I have our five hundred pounds before the day's end, one way or the other."

It was useless of Emily to protest that her curls would mean nothing to Lord Carrigan, that he would not even recognize them, and that even if he did, he would not pay five hundred pounds for the return of the former owner of them. So excited was Lady Randolph by the brilliance of her latest notion, that she insisted that they go upstairs at once to tell Tanker all about it.

"And if you try to get away," she warned Emily as they went into the hall and toward the stairs, "your friend, the footman, will be in for it."

But when they reached the room upstairs, a far different sight greeted their eyes than what they had expected to see. Mr. Tanker was no longer in possession of his rusty pistol. Indeed, he was no longer standing on his feet. Certainly, he was not guarding a footman, or anyone else, for that matter. Bound and gagged with pieces of his own shirt, he lay rolled, like a hedgehog in winter, in a corner of the empty chamber.

"Oh, Herbert!" Lady Randolph cried. "I declare you've gone and let him get away!"

An open window gave evidence that she could not have thought of a truer thing to say.

CHAPTER TWENTY

Just at that moment, to Emily's relief and Lady Randolph's obvious dismay, there came the sound of pounding on the door downstairs, followed by the shattering of glass, and, in a moment, there was the sound of steps everywhere below, and then on the stairs. Bert was the first to burst into the room, closely followed by a contingent that included Emily's father, Lord Nicholson, and Lord Carrigan. Emily threw herself into the Squire's arms to be soundly kissed.

"I didn't know if it was right or wrong to leave you, Miss," Bert declared. "But I thought you could hold your own with Her Ladyship here, and I was afraid she'd find a way to fly the coop unless she was surrounded, so to speak."

"Well, Lola?" Lord Nicholson demanded with a furious air. "What have you to say for yourself? Are you and this fellow behind the kidnappings? Why, damme, if it isn't Tanker. You always told me he was your business representative."

"That and a bit more, I fancy, Milord," Bert replied, clearly quite unwilling to sink back into the subservience of his footman's role. "From what me and Miss Brooke here overheard, they were plotting to raise the money to retire on."

"It is not quite as simple as that," Lady Randolph declared defiantly. "If you must know, Lord Nicholson, the kidnappings was planned by the young gentlemen themselves. All three of them. And I intend that you confront them and let them deny it if they can."

"Confront them?" Lord Carrigan said. "You mean to discontinue your plot then?"

Emily realized that he had not looked directly at her since entering the room. No doubt, he thought she had acted foolishly in coming here alone with Bert. And, indeed, if she had used her head, she would have sent Bert to them directly and let them take charge as gentlemen always should. Instead, she had been precipitate, and it was only thanks to Bert's cleverness that she was not in real trouble now.

"*I* was ready to discontinue the plot, as you put it, a good while ago," Lady Randolph declared, looking down her long nose. "And if everyone had behaved as they should, I would have done so, even if Tanker *was* keen on going on."

At this, Tanker began to put up as great a hue and cry as is possible for someone bound hand and foot, and gagged to boot, and Bert suggested that he be allowed to release him.

"I've had it done enough times to me to know it's not the most comfortable position to be in," he said, but Lady Randolph placed herself directly in front of the unfortunate Tanker and gave it as her opinion that matters could be cleared up much more readily if she were spokesman for the two of them, a suggestion to which Tanker responded with muffled roars of frustration.

"I know your ways, Lola," Lord Nicholson warned her, advancing with a beetled brow. "Don't think for a single moment that we are prepared to swallow a cock-and-bull story about the kidnappings not being your idea. I should have known something was up when I found you nosing around that boy of mine."

The actress stood, arms akimbo, and threw her turbaned head back to eye him defiantly. "That boy of yours is a scoundrel, sir," she said, "as much a young no-good as anyone I have ever met, which is to say a very great deal indeed."

"I'm not about to argue with you," Lord Nicholson grumbled. "I know enough about him to have let him stew a bit in this predicament, hoping that it would do his character some good. Of course, I did not know at the time that you and your friend Mr. Tanker were responsible, else I would have sent the ransom money directly, knowing how you bungle things."

The actress seemed to bristle. "No wonder your son finds you disagreeable, sir!" she told him. "This stunt of kidnapping was meant by him to be a small revenge for the meager way in which you dole out his allowance. It was one night at Ranelagh Gardens—the night he disappeared—that we were all sitting about drinking, and he had this idea. I knew at once we shouldn't get mixed up in it, but Tanker *would* insist we lend a hand."

"For a fee, of course," Lord Nicholson said grimly, as Tanker put up a renewed struggle on the floor.

"You don't think we was to do it free, do you?" Lady Randolph replied. "I've never known of you to do naught for nothing, sir, and I've more of a reason than you have for wanting a reward."

"I take it from your general attitude, Madam, that everything did not go precisely as planned," Lord Carrigan intervened, before an open quarrel should break out between the two old acquaintances. "Perhaps you could explain."

How cool his bearing was, Emily thought, still with her father's arm about her. He was a fashionable, London cynic, giving the impression that nothing he might hear would faze him much. And yet there was a hidden force about his manner that made it clear that he intended to have his way. She would not like to be in Lady Randolph's shoes, she thought, if any further harm had come to his brother in this escapade.

"It was your failure to pay directly, which set the trouble off, sir," Lady Randolph said, rounding on Lord Nicholson. It was clear that, forced into a corner and made to tell her story, she was remembering the past few days with fury. One would have thought from her manner that *she* had been wronged.

"I've told you that I thought I might teach the young scoundrel a lesson," Lord Nicholson replied. "It is a notion of his that I will care of any problem that confronts him, and I fancied I might let him dangle for a day or two."

"But they might have killed him, sir!" the Squire protested. "Did you pause to think of that, eh?"

"I am not the one on trial here!" Lord Nicholson bellowed.

"And neither am I, sir, I'm sure," Lady Randolph reported. "I do not have to tell you any of this, including where your son is."

Lord Carrigan scowled. Seldom had Emily ever seen such a dark expression on his face. "I am impatient with word games and petty quarrels," he said. "If you will not give us a straight story, Madam, perhaps your companion will."

"No, no!" Lady Randolph protested. "I prefer to tell it my own way. The agreement was that young Nicholson should come to stay with Tanker and me, and that the note would be sent, the money supplied directly, everyone involved have a tip, and the bulk go to the victim, who would then make his way home as though just released."

"But instead?" Lord Carrigan demanded, cutting off Lord Nicholson and the Squire. "Tell us what happened instead."

The afternoon light pouring through the grimy window of the upstairs room was not kind to Lady Randolph's face, and the girlish shawl hung about her in a dejected manner. Emily sensed that her layer of defiance might be thinner than the gentlemen imagined, and, quite unexpectedly, she felt a wave of sorrow for this woman, who, at worst, was probably guilty of little more than greed and poor sense. If her aunt and Phoebe were here, she reflected, no doubt they would go about putting Lady Randolph at her ease and soon have everyone believing that everything that had happened was for the best.

"Well, sir," the actress told the young Viscount, making a point of ignoring the Duke, "your brother and young Fairfield went off on their respective ways, thinking it all a great lark, and young Nicholson came home with us, just as we had planned. He dictated the letter to his father, and Tanker wrote it, demanding that the five hundred pounds be left at a certain place by sunup the next day. And, when it wasn't there, young Nicholson claimed that he would never have had such an idea if he hadn't been drinking and that he wanted to forget it."

With a great effort, Tanker had managed to chew through his gag, and now he spat it on the floor. "He changed his mind after I'd written that letter and Lola and me had put ourself in a suspicious situation if the Bow Street Runners ever got on our track!" Tanker declared vehemently. "What I said to Lola is that we'd come so far, we might as well go the rest of the way. The only danger was the other lads talking. So, after we brought our young friend here and locked him in the cellar—"

"In the cellar!" Emily cried. "Is that where they are now? Where they all are?"

"We might as well admit it, Tanker, since you can be certain they will check and see," Lady Randolph said in a disgusted manner. "Their whereabouts was the only ace we had, and you threw it away directly, didn't you, you fumblefist! What pocket is the key in? No need to have them try to break the door down. This isn't our property, after all."

"I think that we should be in possession of the facts first," Lord Carrigan said calmly. "I am increasingly inclined to agree with you, Lord Nicholson, in thinking that whatever has happened to them cannot be punishment enough."

"If what this lady says is true, I would agree," the Squire declared.

"After that, Tanker and I began to wonder how we could keep the other two gentlemen from talking," Lady Randolph went on, apparently more than eager now to get the story out. "They had been in their cups, you see, like Nicholson, and we were afraid that when they sobered up—to call a spade a spade—they would let the whole story spill."

"That was why you pretended to be an old friend of my aunt's and came to be her guest," Emily said in a low voice.

"Precisely," the actress said. "Young Fairfield had said enough about his mother and his sister so that I knew the ruse would work. But I had not expected to find you there. I was taking a risk and well I knew it. No doubt you may say I could have sent a letter. But we thought my constant presence would serve as a reminder and, at the same time, I would be better placed to nip any defection in the bud."

"You make it all sound quite reasonable," Lord Nicholson growled, hovering over her in his bearlike way. "But how do you explain their being beaten to within an inch of their lives? How do you explain that, eh?"

"That was a mistake, sir," Bert declared. At his ease now, with the rusty pistol sticking in the pocket of his livery, he was clearly enjoying himself. "When Miss Brooke and I was standing in the hallway downstairs and listening to these two, we heard it all explained."

"We only meant their feathers to be ruffled a little as a warning," Tanker muttered. He had managed to work himself into an upright position and was leaning against the wall with a plaintive expression on his broad face.

"A warning not to give you away?" Lord Carrigan demanded.

"That's all it was meant to be, sir," Lady Randolph declared. "Tanker and I was watching, and when we saw that they were really being beaten, I thought it the better part of wisdom to leave Lady Fairfield's house."

"And the next day?" the young Viscount urged her. "That is to say today. How did my brother and young Fairfield fall into your clutches?"

"It was the best way to see that they kept quiet," Tanker grumbled. "We never meant 'em any harm."

"All the same, it was stupid! Stupid!" Lady Randolph cried. "I said so at the time! What did we need with three of them? We should have let Nicholson go and taken a little trip on the Continent. I've always wanted to go abroad."

"You nit!" Tanker exploded. "Can't you keep it in that peabrain of yours that we do not have money? Since you were let go from your last engagement—"

"I did not come here to witness a domestic quarrel!" Lord Nicholson declared, in a voice that seemed to rock the building. "Although I must say that you have my deepest sympathies, Mr. Tanker. I had forgotten how exasperating she can be. But how *did* you lure the two lads here? Lads I call them! Rapscallions would be a better word."

"I wrote to Lord Carrigan's brother this morning and told him to let young Fairfield know that unless both of them met me at a certain spot on the Mall this morning, it would be the worse for their friend," Lady Randolph said, with an attempt at renewed dignity after Tanker's attack. "I knew that, after they had been beaten so the night before, they would take the threat seriously. And they did."

"We told them Nicholson wanted to see them," Tanker muttered. "And so I expect he did, having been alone in that cellar for the past few days."

"It only has been two," Emily said reflectively.

"I assure you it seems a good deal longer, my dear," Lady Randolph assured her. "I never have been so nervously exhausted in my entire life, even when I played Gerty Gigs at the Apollo."

"Why don't one of you call the constables," Tanker suggested. "It's a relief to have it over, I can tell you that. Show a little feeling, Lola, and unwind me. Damme, I've lost all feeling in my legs, see if I haven't!"

"That's all right, Madam," Bert declared as Lady Randolph hesitated. "I tied these knots, and I'm the one should untie them."

Meanwhile, Lord Nicholson turned to face the company. "In honor of old times," he began and paused to clear his throat, "in honor of old times and knowing that Lola always was a nitwit, I propose we leave the constables out of it. I mean to say, if what they report is true, our three young relations have a good deal to answer for. This experience may be the making of them, 'pon my soul."

"But do you think those two are to be believed?" the Squire said, nodding in the direction of Tanker, who was groaning as he stretched his legs out straight, while the actress told him that it was all his fault.

"I think they are," Emily said in a clear voice. "No doubt Lord Carrigan will think I am naive, but I have decided that being such is better than being cynical, if one must make the choice. I believe their story, for two less likely criminals I do not think I have ever seen."

She started when Lord Carrigan touched her arm and indicated that they might speak in private. As soon as they were alone in the corner of the room, he spoke in a low voice.

"They did manage to make a botch of it," he told her, "and as for thinking you naive, I think, on the contrary, that you have been very brave and sensible, Miss Brooke. Indeed, I am prepared to list any number of other virtues, if sometime you will agree to sit down with me to listen to them."

He smiled a slow smile and his eyes played the tease with hers. Emily knew that she was blushing, but she found she did not care.

"The first time we met, sir," she replied, "I would not listen to what you had to say. But now, I can assure you I will attend to every word."

CHAPTER TWENTY-ONE

Declaring that his son's incarceration had done him all the good in the world and that he had been transformed, through sheer fright, into an upstanding young fellow, Lord Nicholson celebrated the metamorphosis by holding an elaborate soiree, consisting of an entertainment starring the actress and comedian, Lola Hewlett, followed by a supper and concluded by a midnight masquerade.

"La, my dear Miss Hewlett!" Lady Fairfield exclaimed as she loaded her plate with tarts and sweetmeats from the supper buffet. "I declare you made me laugh until I thought I should roll off my seat, indeed you did."

"One time, I had to hold you upright, Mama," Phoebe exclaimed, making a foray into a dish of strawberry cream. "And I was laughing so myself, I thought I might not be able."

The actress acknowledged these honest accolades with the slipside smile of one who has made an encounter hitherto avoided. She was still wearing the costume she had chosen for her comic part, consisting of a short gown, which was white in back and black in front and decorated all over with red dots that matched the color of her stockings. Her hair had miraculously turned from orange to jet black overnight, and what part of her face as could be seen from underneath her half-mask was charmingly decorated with every means of artifice known to woman.

"Delightful!" Lady Fairfield said, still referring to the entertainment. "I wish I had seen you perform before, Miss Hewlett. It is a strange thing that, although I am certain I have never seen you on the stage before this night, there is something familiar about you."

"I think so, too, Mama," Phoebe declared. "You will recall that I commented on it during the performance."

"My Lola takes a great many people that way," Mr. Tanker declared, appearing out of nowhere and taking the actress by the arm. "I dare say, ladies, it comes of playing so many parts. In the end, there's a touch about her of everyone."

And, with this unlikely exclamation, he bore her off with her plate half-filled as she protested loudly.

"Lord Nicholson has such a range of friends," Phoebe observed, "quite democratic. At least, that was how it struck me when our Bert received an invitation. Why, I was not even aware that the Duke had ever met him."

"It has something to do with Jeremy's rescue, I think," Lady Fairfield said, helping herself to an oyster patty. "I am so glad no one insisted on giving us the details. Much better not to know, I think."

"Oh, yes, Mama. I do so agree. Only look! There is syllabub as well!"

"And there is Bert, I think," Lady Fairfield said, inclining her turban in the direction of the dance floor, where lines were forming for the first cotillion. "He has his domino on, so I cannot be certain. But he is wearing that blue satin coat of Jeremy's I had let out for him."

"Oh, yes, of course!" Phoebe replied. "I know for certain that it is Bert, because that is Nelly with him. See how well pink silk suits her, although perhaps it should have been taken in a deal more about the waist."

"Let me help you to some pickled salmon, my dear Miss Fairfield," Sir Adrian Rap declared, mincing up beside Phoebe and making a proper bow. "The Duke will take it as a slight if we do not make a proper meal of it. You know how quick he is to take offense."

It had been the Duke's unique idea to break the custom of having his guests sit down to supper in one room and to go in to dancing in another. As a consequence, the entire party was together in the elegant ballroom, with its Doric columns and long windows draped with red satin, all lighted by a thousand candles blazing from five great chandeliers. The musician's platform was at one end of the ballroom and the buffet table, ladened with delicacies, was set in a commodious alcove opposite. Nothing was lacking to create a festive atmosphere as bottles popped and ladies' laughter tinkled and the scent of roses filled the air.

"You know we do not know the details, Sir Adrian," Lady Fairfield said, pausing to make a little buzzing sound of pleasure when she saw the green mint charlotte covered with whipped cream, "about Jeremy's rescue, I mean, but I am certain that you must have played a part in it."

"Oh, yes!" Phoebe exclaimed. "When we first found that he was missing and you set off at once to see your friends among the magistrates and other important people, I felt quite confident that my brother would be returned in no time, which turned out to be true!"

"However can we thank you?" Lady Fairfield asked him. "Our savior! I do not think I go too far in saying that."

"Oh, no, Mama!" her daughter exclaimed.

"No doubt, we will have occasion to show our gratitude more properly when Sir Adrian has had another opportunity to speak to my brother privately," Lady Fairfield suggested, and a look of mutual understanding passed between mother and daughter.

"Oh, as for that," Sir Adrian declared, tugging at his cravat nervously, "I think that I have changed my mind."

"What's that?" Lady Fairfield cried, her smile flickering like a candle almost ready to go out.

"Oh, dear!" Phoebe exclaimed, forgetting the plate and the heaped buffet entirely.

"I hope it does not give you that much displeasure, Lady Fairfield," Sir Adrian declared, "to know that I would like to offer to make your daughter my wife."

"Displeasure!" Lady Fairfield cried so loudly that the musicians stopped their tuning and the company turned in her direction.

"Oh, Mama!" Phoebe cried, making a general collapse in every direction, with the result that the Squire, who was passing, rushed to take her plate.

"My apologies, dear ladies!" Sir Adrian exclaimed, hiding behind his quizzing-glass. "I should have done this privately. Never fear. I understand your displeasure."

"Displeasure!" Lady Fairfield cried.

"Oh, Mama!" Phoebe repeated. "Oh, dear Sir Adrian!"

Sir Adrian took a few mincing steps around her. "Miss Fairfield!" he declared. "Do you mean to tell me that I can dare to hope?"

"That is precisely what I think she means, sir," the Squire said, laughing. "Well, sir. My congratulations. I like nothing better than to see people happy. Come, Jeremy. It seems your sister is affianced. What have you to say?"

There was little about Jeremy to recall the fop of the days before. His sojourn in the cellar of the house on Dill Street had been short in the extreme, but, perhaps because he did not know any better than the others how long he would be incarcerated, and because of a certain distaste for rats and vermin, he had been shocked from his complacency into the plain and proper life.

"I only hope Sir Adrian will become less of a man about town," he said now in a cautionary manner that matched the dull brown of his costume and the neat side curls of his hair. "If he is to settle down, he must do it properly. But, no doubt, that is his intention."

"Why, I hope that he intends to do no such thing!" Phoebe declared. "Indeed, I like him just the way he is, the perfect gentleman!"

From their place in the bower of one of the windows, Emily and Lord Carrigan observed this little drama. They had remained silent, since he had joined her there some time ago, silent and apparently intent on watching the scenes that took place around them. It was as though they had made a compact to see life from the same vantage point in order to come to some conclusion.

"Will they be happy, do you think?" Emily said now, nodding to the spot beside the table where Sir Adrian smirked and Phoebe beamed in response to congratulations. Lady Fairfield, who had taken her brother's arm, was shining like a setting sun.

"He cannot get enough of the world as it really is, with all its scandal and cruelty," Lord Carrigan replied slowly. "And your cousin wants to see nothing but good. It may well prove a disastrous union."

"Not if they love one another, surely," Emily replied, glancing at him wistfully.

Lord Carrigan shrugged his broad shoulders. "Perhaps,"

he said in a low voice. "People never cease to amaze. Did my brother make his apologies to you?"

"He did," Emily said with a sigh. "I do not know how it is, but the change in him seems sad, just as it does in Jeremy."

"Why, as for that," Lord Carrigan said dryly, "I rather think this new soberness will not take long to wear itself off. At least, that is my opinion. No doubt, it will come as a shock to Lord Nicholson, but I believe they will be up to their old tricks presently."

"You *are* a cynic, sir," she told him. "Has no one ever surprised you and been better than you thought?"

The young Marquess hesitated and, as he did so, the footman, Bert, put in an appearance, with Nelly by his side.

"We want your advice, Miss," Bert declared, pulling his mask aside. "At least, Nelly says we do, and I do not know as there is anyone whose word I would rather take, unless it was yours, Lord Carrigan."

"The fact is, Miss," the abigail said, all in a rush, "I take it as an omen, our being here. And now Miss Phoebe's engagement announced! 'We've kept it a secret too long, Bert,' I told him, 'and I'm certain that the others will feel the same.'"

"By that, you mean the other servants?"

"Yes, Miss. For months, we've been robbing Lady Fairfield blind. Mrs. Burbain has been selling off the surplus food she bought on credit, and I have been pawning my mistress's jewelry in order to get ready cash."

"And I have been renting out her carriage when I knew she would not require it," Bert declared.

Emily could not see Lord Carrigan's eyes because he had replaced his domino, but she could guess at his expression. Doubtless, this would only go to reinforce his general view of humanity.

"The point is, Miss," Nelly was saying, "that we did it to provide a nest egg for her to serve when the bills were as overdue as could be allowed."

"The merchants will come down on her any day now," Bert declared, "but we are ready for them. The only problem being—"

"How to make arrangements in a way which will mean

she'll not be troubled," Nelly finished for him. "And I thought, Miss, that you might have the answer for us."

Emily could not resist throwing her arms about them both in turn, while Lord Carrigan removed his domino and stared at them with puzzled eyes.

"I knew there must be an answer to the puzzle," Emily declared, "for it was plain to me you cared for her. What an extraordinary thing for you to do!"

"She *would* spend every shilling which was at hand," the footman said with a black smile. "She cannot help her nature. We only meant to retrieve what we could of it."

"We have a tidy sum, Miss," Nelly said proudly. "But what the next step should be, we are not certain."

"I think the answer to that has just come in the door," Emily replied. "Leave everything to me, and I will see that Mr. Drew makes the necessary arrangements."

The music struck up at that moment, and footman and abigail whirled away. "Come, sir," Emily said boldly, taking Lord Carrigan's arm. "You will please me by being witness."

The solicitor caught sight of her immediately and hurried across the floor, bringing in his wake an old gentleman, who managed gamely with his cane.

"Lord Harmond!" Emily cried.

"But of course you two know one another!" Mr. Drew exclaimed. "And this, sir, is Lord Carrigan."

"Miss Brooke will have thought me lacking in manners," Lord Harmond declared, looking at her in the same speculative manner he had employed at the time of their first meeting in the library of Lady Courtiney's house. "After all, I did not answer your letter, asking for a meeting."

Emily realized, with a start, that in the excitement of the past few days, she had forgotten the danger into which her father's speculation had thrown them. And now, no doubt, Mr. Drew had brought Lord Harmond with him to tell her that all was lost!

"The fact is, my dear," Lord Harmond said in his creaking voice, "that when I heard from you, I decided to make an investment in your father's name. An investment that I knew I could not lose."

"An abandoned coal mine in Yorkshire," Mr. Drew declared.

"It has a familiar sound," Emily told him, hoping he would not hear the irony in her voice.

"This time I was successful, gel!" the old man told her, rapping the floor with his cane. "That is, the shares I bought for your father already show a fine profit. Damme, more than that! It is a boom! Profits piling up in every direction!"

"We came to tell the Squire!" Mr. Drew exclaimed. "It is a piece of good news that will not wait."

"You will find him in that direction," Emily said, bending forward to kiss the old gentleman on one withered cheek.

"Damned lucky fellow, that Carrigan," she heard him mutter, and then he was off, propelled across the dance floor, which was beginning now to be filled with couples for the gavotte.

"You see, sir," Emily declared, turning to Lord Carrigan, "there are all sorts of well-intentioned people about. And, sometimes, as my aunt would say, things do come right in the end."

Lord Carrigan was smiling now, and there were no shadows to haunt his dark eyes or his face.

"I think things will always come right for me as long as you are with me," he told her.

And then the music swelled and she was in his arms, bringing an end to all talk about philosophy. The fortune wheel had turned again.

From bestselling author
PATRICIA HAGAN

Four magnificent epics that rip across the tumultuous landscapes of the Civil War—and the embattled terrains of the heart!

PASSION'S FURY   77727 $2.95

Rance Taggert, a dashing and irresistible scoundrel wins lovely
April Jennings in a reckless bet. Yet even in her determination
to return to her plantation home she cannot forget Rance . . .
for though she might escape him, he has won her heart forever!

SOULS AFLAME   75507 $2.75

As the shadow of the Civil War hangs over her homeland, Julie
Marshall sets sail on a blockade-running frigate bound for
London. Together with the brooding, mysterious Captain Derek
Arnhardt, she discovers a passion neither can control, tempting
fate and enemy cannons from Bermuda to Savannah, till they
can seal at last the love that has set their souls aflame!

LOVE AND WAR   77206 $2.95

Lovely, golden-haired Katherine Wright, wrenched from her
plantation home, finds herself abducted, fighting for her life—
and for the freedom to choose the man she will love: Nathan
Collins, the Rebel; or Travis Coltrane, the Yankee who makes
her wild with fury one moment and delirious with passion the next.

THE RAGING HEARTS   46201 $2.75

As the War draws to a close, Kitty Wright's ancestral home
stands abandoned and ruined, and two carpetbaggers prepare
to turn their hunger to her beauty. But Kitty will surrender to no
man until a special one from her past returns—a victorious
soldier who knows that a man's greatest field of honor is a
woman's heart!

BESTSELLING ROMANCE
by Johanna Lindsey

PARADISE WILD   77651 $2.95

From high-bred Boston society to the wilder shores of Hawaii's blazing tropical sands, an impetuous beauty and a man of smoldering anger meet head-on in a battle of wills, revenge and love. Corinne Barrows and Jared Burkett find a love so violent, so reckless, that it must either destroy them—or give them completely to the wild abandon of tropical nights in paradise!

FIRES OF WINTER   75747 $2.50

Abducted from Ireland across an icy sea, the lovely and dauntless Lady Brenna vows vengeance on her Viking captors. Though slavery is the fate of women captured on raids, Brenna swears she will never be owned. But the Viking leader Garrick claims her, and between them is forged a bond of desire—until a rival Norseman challenges Brenna to defy Garrick, whom she despises as a master . . . but loves as a man.

A PIRATE'S LOVE   75960 $2.50

From sun-blazed beaches to star-lit coves, languid Caribbean breezes sweep a ship westward, carrying the breathtakingly beautiful Bettina Verlaine to fulfill a promise her heart never made—marriage to a Count she has never seen. Then the pirate Tristan captures Bettina's ship. Many days—and fiery nights —pass, while he casts his spell over her heart, and their passion blossoms into the fragile flower a woman can give to only one man.

CAPTIVE BRIDE   75978 $2.50

Recklessly following her brother from London to Cairo, beautiful Christina Wakefield is abducted by an unknown stranger who carries her off to his hidden encampment, where she is made his prisoner. There she shares his bed, learns to know his touch, and grows ever closer to the man who owns her as a slave. And soon she learns to want the desert sheik as he wants her—and to submit to a stormy and passionate love.

Available wherever paperbacks are sold, or directly from the publisher. Include 50¢ per copy for postage and handling: allow 6–8 weeks for delivery. Avon Books, Mail Order Dept., 224 West 57th St., N.Y., N.Y. 10019.

(Lindsey 8-81) (1-B)